Carol Macfie Lange is Scottish, has a BA in Theatre Arts/Santa Fe New Mexico, Masters in English/Westminster College Oxford, produced theatre in Greece, Spain, Germany, New Mexico and UK, lived 22 years in Andalucia Spain, published two novels in a trilogy about the Spanish Civil War: *Invisible Child* and *Green on Snow*, and a children's book, and now lives in Oxford with family.

"This book had me gripped from start to finish. It is beautifully written, with stunning descriptions that I actually had to read aloud to bask in the poetry of the language. The characters are well defined and easy to associate with. None of them are black and white, each having in-depth back stories that gave deeper dimension to their personalities.

This book taught me a lot about Franco's reign and made me interested enough to research the history behind the book. It is a stark and horrifying history, which is well represented in this book with some truly unnerving and sickening depictions of cruelty.

The tone of the book reminded me of one of my favourite novels. Two Brothers by Ben Elton, in the way it developed each character's story and how they crossed paths in a time of great repression and persecution. What this book managed to do more successfully than the Elton novel was to weave a story that was gripping and emotional beyond the time period it took place in. The events and characters were good in their own right and I was absorbed by what was happening in their interactions, instead of merely dragging myself through a disturbing depiction of horrors.

I was very impressed with the quality of the writing, the use of language and the story development, which I believe to be the first in a series. If so, I can't wait to get my hands on the second (especially as the ending packed one of the biggest punches I've read in a long time.)"

DM Cain, author *The Phoenix Project*

"This book was a fascinating and beautifully written read. I mostly enjoyed the way Carol Macfie Lange gets under the skin of her characters, making them very believable. The story had me gripped from the first page and stayed with me long after I'd finished. If you are looking for a book that is guaranteed to hold your interest, look no further. I look forward to reading more of Ms. Lange's books."

Tarian Green, author *The Tethered Unicorn*

BY THE SAME AUTHOR

NOVELS
Invisible Child
Green on Snow

CHILDREN
Maya and the Magic Sunflower

ANTHOLOGIES
Double Decker
Tales from the Bookshop
Tales from the Opera
Santa Fe Poetry Forum
South London Courier
Poets' Theatre

SCRIPTS
The Cemetery of Forgotten Women

Angelita's Song

CAROL MACFIE LANGE

Matador
Unit E2 Airfield Business Park
Harrison Road, Market Harborough
Leicestershire LE16 7UL
Tel: 0116 279 2299
Email: books@troubador.co.uk
Web: www.troubador.co.uk/matador
Twitter: @matadorbooks

Editors: Pam Elise Harris and Cristina Garcia Parry

Cover art: Pepa Cobo

ISBN 9781803136974

British Library Cataloguing in Publication Data.
A catalogue record for this book is available from the British Library.

Printed by TJ Books Ltd, Padstow, UK
Typeset in 11pt Minion Pro by Troubador Publishing Ltd, Leicester, UK

Matador is an imprint of Troubador Publishing Ltd

In memory of Rolf

one

I'M EIGHTEEN, AND I'VE ALREADY LOVED A BOY, BEEN in prison and killed a man.

I'll never understand why everyone hates my father. He is always gentle and affectionate with me, his only child. When he was still strong, we would ride together on the plains around Madrid, racing our horses across the distances with wild abandon, leaping over rocks and fallen trees and laughing into the summer winds. He had a fierce energy then, but as the years pass, he is becoming frail, crippled by some invisible agony, his big body ponderous and slow.

As I grow into adulthood, I ache to be with him, care for him, feel my own way in the world, and explore the silence and mysteries of my past. I grasp at freedom, a liberty that offers choice. I know Madrid is dangerous, especially for women. Women have no justice, no choice or freedom. Over the years, a seed of rage grows in me as I discover that the dictator Franco has made this happen. My mission is to leave the village and go to Madrid to care for my father, oppose Franco, and join the struggle for the rights of women.

I beg my mother to let me leave. She exchanges looks with my big brother, looks that have passed between them over the years with an odd silent acknowledgment that excludes and enrages me. I turn to my brother in mute appeal. He shakes his head, puts his arm around me, kisses the top of my head, and leaves. I adore my big brother and am sure I can trust him, yet no amount of cajoling will make him change his mind.

They come for me at the house while my mother and her husband Orlando are downriver tending the orchard. I have been seen and identified. They take me to the holding house and lock me up. What I have done is unforgivable, the wrecking and poisoning of the river and the harvest, a crime against the community. I want to punish my family and the villagers for all the years of silence, the whispers, the lies and unknown truths.

"You will stay here until we are able to contact the *Alcalde,* who will decide what we must do with you," the first guard says. "I will try to find him now."

The other guard is bearlike, strong, his face and head a tangle of unwashed greasy hair. He sweats profusely, and his breath stinks. He comes into my room, puts his hand on my face, and strokes my cheek. I swipe his hand away. He pushes me against the wall.

"You're sweet," he growls, "sweet and new."

His hands are upon me, all over me, and I feel his groin swell as he presses against me. I try to push him away, but he is too strong. He grasps my dress and lifts it over my hips. I fall to my knees.

"Oh, so that's how you like it!" he rasps.

The bitterness makes me choke, and I clench my teeth. He screams. I reach behind for the baton on his hips, leap to my feet and with all my strength, club him on the back of his head. He falls to the floor, grasping his groin. I go on hitting him until blood appears and he lies still. I fumble for his keys, open the door, and flee.

I rush to my house, stuff a small rucksack with bread and cheese and water, untie the horse, and head for the mountains.

*

I'm almost to the pond before I stop. My body aches from tension and disgust. I can still feel the saliva on my neck. The stink of the man's fingers and the bitter taste of him lingers in my mouth. I raise my face to the sky and howl. It is our signal. Tomas will know I am at the pond. I run to the still crystal water and peel off my clothes. The water feels like a benediction, cool and sweet on my hot body. I gulp spring water, rinse, spit, rinse and spit again and again. I grope to the bank and lie in the sun to dry.

A hand touches my shoulder. I shoot up.

"It's me, *carino*, Tomas. It's all right. What has happened to you?" His face is creased with concern. "No, don't talk now." He lifts me gently and cradles me in his arms. It is an hour before I can speak. I tell him everything. He listens in silence, his black eyes bright with horror and worry.

"You cannot go back," he says. "We don't know if he is dead. But if he is, they will never let you leave. You must stay here with me. You'll be safe here. Nobody knows of this place."

"But your parents…"

He ponders that. "I'll have to think about what to tell them. But my first instinct is that it would be better for you to stay here, at the pond. You are safe here. I can stay with you—"

"I'm going to Madrid," I cut in.

Tomas's eyes grow huge with disbelief. "But… but how? How can you possibly go alone? No. I will go with you."

"I'm going to my father, Tomas. I'll be safe there."

"Yes, but… Madrid… *es lejos… It's too far… How…*"

"And I'm going alone."

Tomas's voice shakes. "Please, Angelita… I'm begging you—"

"Tomas, you are my dearest friend. I love you. I trust you more than anyone in the world. No. Listen to me. Please. Just listen. I must go alone. It is something I have to do." His eyes glisten. I snuggle close to him and touch his face. "Dear Tomas, this is not goodbye. You can come later, but now is not the time."

He is silent for a long time. "I will help you," he says at last. "I will bring food and some clothes of mine. You must not travel as a woman. It is too dangerous. These mountains are not safe, the coast is not safe, and the city is not safe. Not for you. You are beautiful and young, and men will want to own you."

I kiss his cheek. "I know you're right, and I'll do as you suggest. I won't go tonight. Stay here with me tonight, Tomas. Bring the stuff for me, and tomorrow… tomorrow I'll leave for the coast. That way I can get to Malaga and a train to Madrid. Do you have any money?"

He nods. "I'll go now. I'll bring everything tonight. I'll stay and be here before you leave in the morning."

I watch him climb to his mountain. It's like watching a flame go out, and although it is warm in the sun, I shiver. My hands are icy cold. My hands are always freezing when I am afraid or upset. I put my clothes on and wait. Soon Tomas returns. He brings blankets, a cap, shirt and trousers of his own, and thick shoes slightly too big and padded in the toes. Into a leather food bag, he has placed chunks of cheese, sausage and bread, and from his neck dangle two skins of water.

*

I first met Tomas on one of my mountain forays. I often took my horse and rode up into the high mountains. I was twelve, he a year younger. He sat by a spring cupping the crystal water into his hands, drinking thirstily. The morning sun filtered through the olive leaves, glistening on his long obsidian hair as he bent over. I thought he was beautiful, sun-kissed and shining, shaking his long hair down the slim strong back like a water creature. Suddenly, he peeled off his clothes and plunged into the pond, gasping with pleasure. I laughed He glanced round quickly.

"What'd you do if I make off with these?" I grinned, holding up his clothes.

"I'd go home naked," he laughed, "and get a good hiding for losing my clothes. Who are you? It's hot. You should come in."

I peeled off my clothes. The water is cool and soft on my hot skin. I inhaled the sweet aroma of wildflowers on the bank.

"I'm Angelita," I announced, splashing water at him.

Laughing, he splashed back. "Tomas," he says. "I live up there." He pointed to the mountain. "With my parents and three sisters. We are *Gitano,* so we have to be careful. There are Guardia, even up here sometimes."

Tomas is my first real friend as I grow to young womanhood. We fight and care for each other like siblings, with affection, ridicule and trust. We play a game called Truth or Lie, where we take turns sharing secrets we can never tell anyone else. If the other does not believe the story, he or she calls out, "Liar!". It is then up to the teller to convince the other of the truth. If convinced, the listener carves a notch on the ancient chestnut tree behind the pond.

Tomas tells me he killed a soldier and buried him in the chasm. He had been hunting rabbits in the woods not far from the house when he heard heavy footsteps crackling in the branches nearby. He hid behind a tree, peeped out cautiously. The man was a Guardia. Tomas was afraid. He knew Guardia had their orders, that *Gitanos* were targeted by the government and at risk. *Gitanos* were rebellious, independent, high on the list for punishment or death from the Franco regime. Tomas aimed his slingshot. The sharp stone hit the Guardia on the temple. He fell and lay still.

"Liar!" I call out.

Tomas looks at me and quietly continues. He tiptoed close and rolled the Guardia over the rocks into the deep chasm below. He threw branches and rocks on top of the body until it was completely hidden.

We sit in silence for some time.

"I am not ashamed of what I did," he says at last. "I protected my family." A red flush appears on his neck, and he sits very still.

I walk over to the oak tree and carve a notch below his name.

"Your turn," he says. "Truth or Lie." His voice sounds funny, thick and hoarse as if something is stuck in his throat.

"I just have one question," I say. "What happens if I just make it all up?"

"Then you'll be stung to death by bees," he laughs. "And swell up like a dead boar and die."

"But how would you know?" I insist.

"I would know by the look in your eyes. When you make something up, your eyes go flat, but when you tell the truth, they go dark and black and they sparkle and make me want to hug you."

"I tortured a cat," I say abruptly. Angry with my mother for not letting me go to Madrid, I wanted to hurt something. "I put it into a cage and poked at it with sharp sticks. I felt horrible afterwards. That's not nearly as bad as killing someone."

Tomas stares into my eyes. "Did it die?"

"I let it go. It was bleeding. It ran away, and I felt sick. Your turn."

"I've already had two goes. Anyway, I have to carve your notch."

"Let's swim then," I say, peeling off my clothes. We leap into the jade green shade of the pool and swim to the cave on the other side, hidden by prickly wild asparagus. To reach the cave we have to swim round the bushes, dive, and come up inside the cave. We sit in the coolness and open the food pouch with the bread and goat's cheese.

I lie back on a smooth rock. "I love it here. I feel safe here, free."

Tomas gazes at me, suddenly serious. "I want you to promise me something. If you are ever in trouble or need to get away, you'll come here. Only I would know where you were. We must never tell anyone about this place. Swear it."

"I swear," I say solemnly. "You the same."

"Me the same. I swear. Anyway, that'll never happen. We'd never run away. we're happy here."

"You never know." I slap him on the head and dive back under the bush, into the pond. He follows, laughing and gasping, black sleek hair shining like a water creature in the sun. Suddenly, he freezes and raises a finger to his lips.

"Someone is moving in the woods," he whispers.

"I don't hear anything."

"Be still. Wait."

We swim silently to the edge of the pond and wait in the shadows. I grow impatient and make a movement. Tomas holds my arm, shakes his head, and raises his finger again to his lips.

The quiet tread of the *cabra de montana* ceases at the water's edge. It bends its slender head to drink and steps along the edge of the pond, its movements quiet and gentle, a young female, belly swollen with imminent young. A stick cracks on the hill above, and she raises her head, dark eyes huge with alarm. A rifle shot. The doe drops. Two men slide down the hill, haul her up to the top and disappear into the woods. I will never forget the look in her eyes, a dying of the light that would stay with me through the times ahead.

*

"I should cut my hair," I say to Tomas. He reaches and catches one of my curls.

"Just one piece," he says, "for me to keep. Don't cut the rest, just tie it up under the cap. Boys do that sometimes when they want to keep their hair long. Be careful not to take the cap off, just in case." He snips a curl, wraps it carefully in a leaf, places it in his pocket.

We share the bread and sausage and oranges he has brought and drink from the spring. He unwraps a chunk of olive soap and asks if he can wash me.

"I'll be careful. I won't hurt you. I want you to be clean of that bastard."

"Dear Tomas," I whisper.

Leaving next morning is hard. We spend the night in each other's arms and love each other for the first time with a tender, gentle passion we have never known before. In the dim light of the crescent moon, I watch him. I trace his mouth with my finger, and he smiles in his sleep. He looks like a saint.

For the first time in my life, I wait for the sunrise with a heavy feeling of imminent loss.

Together we pack my things into the leather rucksack and stand looking at each other.

"You will not forget," he says.

I swallow, willing back the tears. "Never," I whisper.

We do not—cannot—touch, for if we do, I will not go. He knows it and stands apart, irresolute, face twisted with tightly controlled emotion, then turns and walks away up the mountain without looking back.

When I reach the bottom of the hill, I turn to look back. He sits, shoulders hunched like a small child being punished, unmoving, and gazes down at me, huge black eyes flat and lifeless as a star-starved night. I turn and walk away, my hand on the hollow where my heart is. I force back the sob that rises in my throat. As I reach the edge of the forest and begin the descent to the valley, I hear his wolf howl and howl back.

We know it is a farewell.

two

I DECIDE NOT TO CHANGE INTO MY DISGUISE UNTIL I reach the coast, for I know these trails well and feel safe there. I leave my horse with Tomas and continue on foot, avoiding the villages, listening intently before making my way to the next forest trail. It takes two days to reach the Mediterranean. I nibble sparingly on the food, drink from springs in the forest and fill my water bags. I have a lot of time to think. I think about what I have left behind, and about my father, his frailty, his need of me. I am determined that nothing will stop me from reaching him. I despise those who keep him out of my life, who turn him into a shadow father to visit in dreams and once a year in person. My brother tried to explain to me that he and my father had an agreement: I would be taken to him in Madrid once a year, on the condition that he never again entered the village.

"One day you will understand," my brother tells me gently. "I know you love your father, and that is good. But you must have guessed. Things happened, things he did, unforgivable things, and..."

"I forgive him!" I burst out.

My brother hesitates. "For what? You forgive him for what? You love him for the father he is to you now, but you know nothing of what he was in the past. Our mother—"

"Oh yes, our mother. Of course, you must bring her up because she's the only one in the world who has suffered, isn't she? That's no secret. Everyone in the village tells me so. But that's all they tell me, nothing else. It's as if there's a pact of silence between them!"

"One day you'll know everything, *querida.* when you are older, but not now."

"Oh yes, believe me, one day when I'm old enough, I will leave this village, I don't belong here. I'll go to Madrid and live with my father!"

"That will be your choice," he replies.

That afternoon, he takes me riding down the valley, his hair like golden wings behind him as he rides the valley like a Viking, cradling me in front.

"I love you, little sister," he whispers. "I loved you from the first moment I saw you, so long ago, small and stubborn, fierce and independent even then."

"There's something in me, Izzy, a kind of fire that can't be put out when I know I'm right."

"I know that," he laughs and kisses the top of my head.

I first met my brother when I was six years old, he eighteen. He taught me many things. He taught me that to have a horse obey, you must first love it, stroke it, whisper to it, and care for it. Only then, when it knows you cannot live without it, will it come to you and stay with you forever, not so much subdued as enchanted. Isandro would set me in front of him, tiny and fearless, eyes sparkling, and ride the length of the long green valley until I squealed and sang for joy at the speed and grace of it. It was on those adventures that I first discovered my voice, my love of song. I would make up songs and sing them to the sky.

"You have a beautiful voice, little sister," my brother told me. "And those words, where do they all come from?"

"They come from inside me," I laugh. "I'm full of them! I can't stop them. They just tumble out!"

When I grow older and Isandro leaves the valley, I ride alone, exploring the ridges and chasms of the high mountains, careful to avoid loose terrain that could endanger the horse, singing all the while songs of the mountains and valleys and forests. The songs change as I grow older and learn of the injustices perpetrated by the government, the violence forced upon women, the subjugation, punishment and death of any opposition.

I learn to eavesdrop, sliding silently into rooms where adults are talking. I overhear that my father was a cruel and violent man. I learn that he was a captain in Franco's civil war, has known immense power and used it. All this makes no sense to me. All I have known from him is tenderness.

"The country's going to hell with Franco," a neighbour says.

"It's already gone! Especially for the women! "

"I've heard about the rapes," the other woman says. "Protest, and they chuck you in prison and do what they like with you."

"And Franco has ordered all the brothels closed, but he turns a blind eye to the capturing of young girls and lets them be put them in special places for the generals to use."

"And… not a word, mind you… but that girl Angelita's father, he's the one who puts them there… he… sshhh! Someone's at the door…"

How I hate those women, their lies, their gossip and

subterfuge. I creep away and sob out my rage and frustration. Sometimes, I question my mother, try to get behind her gentle evasions, but she will not budge. I learn to live with the evasions, the unspoken judgments. They say he was hardened to the cries of the innocent and the appeals of women. This is a part of him I do not know. I know only his love, his tenderness, his later fragility, the livid ancient scar upon his face testament to a deeper suffering I can only imagine.

It will be years before I learn the truth.

I was eight years old the first time I stayed with my father in Madrid. For a whole month each year, we'd spend every moment together. Sometimes in the evenings if it was cold, we'd sit before the fire to eat dinner prepared by the servants and tell stories about the past. I loved those evenings. The light from the fire warmed his face, and his eyes shone as he spoke. Especially when he spoke about my mother.

"From the first moment I saw her, I knew I must have her in my life. She was beautiful like you. brave too. There was a light about her. Her hair—"

"Where did you first see her, Papa?"

He hesitates, gazes out at the rushing life of Madrid, and sighs. "It was on an assignment in the countryside." He swallows, stops speaking. I look into his face, see fear there and reach to touch him. He catches my hand and turns to me. "Sometimes, darling, things happen in life, things that seems strange or inexplicable later."

"What kind of things?"

"Complicated things. Like taking care of someone

who doesn't seem to want help. You can do something you thought was for the best, then find out later that you were wrong."

I reach to take his hands in mine.

"Like you take care of me, Papa? Taking me riding and showing me how to love a horse?"

He kisses the top of my head. "Well… something like that." He puts his arm around me. "Your mother was the best thing that ever happened in my life. She loved me, and now I have you to love."

"But if she loved you, why did she leave you? Now you're all alone, and she's happy. It isn't fair. I don't understand."

"Well, *carino,* some things don't seem to make sense, they just have to be accepted."

"But, Papa, how do you forgive her? She left you."

"There's nothing to forgive, *hija.*"

I will never forget the look in his eyes, the love there, the appeal, the terrible aching vulnerability and sadness, like a hurt, small child. I put my arms around him and kissed the long scar on his cheek.

I love him for his pain, his devotion, his need, a need urgent and compelling enough for him to relinquish power and replace it with compassion. That is how I have known him through the years, as I grow to womanhood: tender and fragile, needy and loving. I saw rage in him only once. A neighbour told him that he should not be exposing me to the horrors of the past and should tell me the truth. The transformation in my father was frightening. Face suffused with anger, the long rigid scar a livid red, he cursed the neighbour, struck him and pushed him from the room.

When he returned, he was calm, his face composed. He held me close, smoothed my hair, and kissed the top of my head. "Let's go riding," he says.

For my thirteenth birthday, he bought me a horse, a swift black Andalucian with a long shining mane and a wild nature. My hair streamed behind as I rode him through the parks and plains of the city, two rebellious spirits cleaving together as one.

I am happy and sing often, songs about the blessing of the rains, the burgeoning springtime blossoms, the fury of wild boar protecting their young. Songs also of loneliness, a sense of not belonging, of not being seen, of being able to touch people only through my songs. My childhood freedom to roam and explore the valley and mountains made me strong. I feel I can survive anywhere, even in the wild. The tranquil rhythms lull and comfort me when I am sad, the fierce resurgence and wildness of nature, the feeling of being a part of it, plants a seed of courage in me like a weapon, a weapon others cannot see, something that comes from inside of me and is untouchable.

three

I T TAKES ME TWO DAYS TO REACH THE MEDITERRANEAN.
As I walk towards the coast, words form in my head, and
I sing.

> *Trees like sentinels/shielding the hidden soft flesh/
> revealing shadows/killer blades swathing, searching/
> in the forest of ideas no-one is safe, not the hypocrite
> plying his torturous trade/not the priest concealing lies
> with prayer/not the guerrera squeezing out her truth/
> like a ripe orange/glistening fluid held in the soul/like
> the semen of a lost lover/to bring one day to life.*

I hear a sound below and stop. It's a *jabeline* rooting for food.
When it sees me, it runs off into the undergrowth. I continue
warily on my way.

Darkness melts into grey and a luminous purple-golden
dawn rises over the sea as I stumble down the final slope,
carefully avoiding the coastal village of Adra.

I learn quickly that here at the coast is another kind of
danger. I join the crowded dusty road to Malaga. People
are hot, exhausted, desperate, flinging themselves into the
sea, drinking the water and retching. I rest on a rock by the
beach and watch the streaming people. A small girl lets go

16

of her mother's hand and comes over to me, her eyes gazing longingly at the food bag by the rock. I reach into the bag and pull out a chunk of bread.

"Eat," I say gently. The child stares at the bread, grasps it, tears off a piece with her teeth and eats hungrily, picking precious crumbs out of the sand. She runs back to her mother. The woman comes over and sits beside me on the rock.

"You are headed in the wrong direction, *nena*," she tells me. "Malaga has been bombed. It is not safe for a woman."

"I have to find my cousins, if they're still there. I need to get a train to Madrid." It's no use telling her that Almeria City is also being bombed, that people have fled inland for safety.

The woman holds a water skin towards me. I hesitate, knowing how scarce water is, and sip briefly, the liquid warm and soothing on my tongue.

A rumbling fills the distance. People fling themselves to the roadside. The child sits unaware, picking crumbs from the dusty road and sucking them. Her mother has moved ahead, holding out her hand behind, calling urgently to the child to come quickly. I throw myself beside the rock and bury my face in the sand.

The air shrieks, a beast in pain and fury, as the planes streak along the lines of prone bodies. As suddenly as they came, they are gone. Some people stumble to their feet, others lie immobile. In the pock-marked road a hand appears here, a leg there, in a grotesque mosaic of human parts. I look for the little girl. To my astonishment, she still sits in the dust, oblivious, picking and sucking on the bread. Her mother has vanished. Some way ahead, a large crater has opened in the road, and people make their way carefully around it.

A beautiful young *Gitana*, black eyes and long obsidian hair gleaming in the sun, sits down unceremoniously beside me.

"That was a good thing you did. The kid," she says abruptly. "I had three, two boys and a girl, all gone back in Malaga. Bombed. The *fascistas* shot my husband after they made him watch me being raped."

She speaks as if telling an anecdote, matter-of-factly, without emotion. I realize she is traumatized, catatonic.

"What is your name?" I ask quietly.

"They call me La Loca, for the crazy way I dance."

I smile gently. "They call me Angelita. They say I sing, like a little angel. Maybe we can dance and sing together."

La Loca grins. "It's good to laugh again. I feel I've been locked away somewhere for the past month with no key."

I look at the long lines of people moving as in a nightmare, then at the sky. They will be back before long, no doubt. I tremble. An acrid smell of smoke or blood permeates the air. Beads of moisture form like tears on my palms.

I try to warn the people. "Almeria is not safe. It has been bombed. People are fleeing." Men and women stare at me blankly, incuriously, shake their heads and move stolidly on towards the city not yet visible in the distance. I realize they have no idea of what is happening there. I know. Tomas warned me of it.

"Do not go near Almeria city. It is in chaos," he'd said. "My cousin was there. Whole families who survived the trek from Malaga are sleeping in the streets, in doorways, on the beaches. Abandoned children drink from the ocean and are sick. Palm leaves, bougainvillea, anything that looks edible, are boiled in sea water to make glutinous stews. An old man sold chunks of bread from a filthy bag around his neck, the price too high for most."

The ancient Andalucian tradition of sharing with the needy has been forgotten. Theft is the accomplice of starvation.

I turn to La Loca. "Look, I think we should go inland, away from here. This road is going nowhere."

"But where? The *campo?* That's where the Guardia find most of the young women for Franco's generals. Fresh, innocent."

"I know a place."

"But the kid? We can't just leave her. Her mother's gone."

We walk over to where the child still sits in the dust. I sit down beside her. "What do they call you?" I ask gently.

"I am Maria del Mar," she replies.

I get up and take her hand. "Well, Maria of the Sea," I smile, "we'd like you to come with us, where it is safe, and there is bread."

Maria del Mar looks up at me quizzically. "Mama?"

"Mama had to move on," La Loca says carefully. "So we'll take care of you." Gently she takes the child's other hand.

And so it is that the three of us: a runaway, a madwoman, and an orphan, all equal in pain and loss, hold hands and head for the mountains.

*

It takes us three days to reach the pond. We have to move more slowly and carefully with the child to help her over obstacles. Her thin spindly legs tremble with effort. She is not used to the mountains. Her whole young life has been spent in Malaga City among *Gitanos*, protected and secure. She is afraid of the night sounds, the rustlings of animals fleeing or seeking food and the sudden surging of the great eagle owls terrify her. We comfort her and are patient. At night, we roll her into the warm blanket Tomas has given me. I sing her to sleep, melodies I remember from my mother, others of my own.

As soon as we reach the hill leading to the pond, I howl. La Loca and the child look at me in alarm.

"It's all right," I assure them. "That's the signal. I'm letting Tomas know we are nearly at the pond."

I have told them a little about Tomas, our childhood friendship and games, our affection for each other. La Loca is skeptical.

"But can we trust him? We have never met him. He may not like us. Two more mouths to feed. And what about his family?"

"They are good people, a big family, *Gitanos* like you both. They know the threat your people live under from the government. They've lived in these mountains for decades and survived the madness coming out of Madrid. You will see. They know these forests and mountains well and live off wild fruits and meat from wild boar and deer. When you meet Tomas, you will understand."

La Loca looks unconvinced.

"Be patient. You can trust me, *amiga*. I promise you will soon see what I'm talking about."

It is unsurprising that La Loca finds it difficult to trust anyone. I recall what she told me about the loss of her children, her husband's murder, and her violation at the hands of the fascists. But I see her begin to change. Over the two days we have spent in the mountains, she has started falling asleep without sitting up in alarm at every sound. I ask about her parents and siblings. That is a mistake. She falls silent and will not speak for an hour. Later, she tells me they have all been lost in the Malaga bombing. Her face takes on the catatonic look I first saw at the beach, and her hands shake as she recalls the images of dismemberment and death. I make a mental note not to ask questions and to let her come forward when she is ready.

She does not like to be touched. When once I put my hand on her arm, she jumped to her feet and walked away. Through the trees, I could see her writhing, frenetic movements as she danced away the horror and sorrow of her loss. Whenever she dances, she is like a thing possessed, her body and lovely arms caressing or accusing the space around her, inviting, cajoling, rejecting in a whirl of passion, beads of sweat forming unheeded as her intense gaze focuses on a world only she can see. This gift, this ability to bring forth tears, adulation and awe in others, would later become our salvation.

It is not long before Tomas appears. He flies down the mountain like a lynx.

"What has happened?" he pants. "I was sure you'd be well on your way to Madrid by now! Was there trouble by the coast? In Malaga? I hadn't heard anything… Doesn't matter… You're here now… safe." He stops, gulps for breath, looks at La Loca and the child. "Who are your friends? You all look exhausted. I've brought some food, I'll get more…"

Dear Tomas, dear and loving friend. "There was a bombing. This is La Loca and little Maria del Mar." I sit down, suddenly aware of how tired I am. The others flop beside me, the trauma and tension of the experience engraved on their faces.

"We must rest, Tomas. Then I'll tell you about my plans."

"Plans? Oh, never mind, *gracias a Dios*, you're here now. You can stay here, all of you. You are safe here. We will take care of you."

"Can we talk later, Tomas? We need time to swim, rest, and eat. Give us a day, then I'll tell you."

I see that he is worried. At the mention of plans, his face turns white. He knows how stubborn I am, how determined. But he stops talking and gets out fresh sausage, cheese, and corn bread still warm from the oven. We eat ravenously and drink from the crystal spring.

"It feels like heaven here," sighs Maria del Mar, her small thin body pressed into the warm ground. "I could stay here forever, just eating and lying in the sun and… let's go for a swim!" And with the impetuous glee of childhood, she peels off her clothes and leaps into the pond.

"It's so good to see her like this," I say to Tomas. "She's been through a lot. Lost her family, her mother, down by the coast."

"She can stay here," he repeats.

La Loca has not spoken. Now she looks at us, eyes huge and black. "I have to go with you, Angelita, to Madrid. But I'm afraid."

Tomas puts out his hand to reassure her. I catch his eye and quickly shake my head. He withdraws his hand and sits still, watching the child.

"Let's just enjoy this day," I say. "Let's think of nothing but the trees, the cool water, the sun on our faces, and friends, and being free."

We spend the whole afternoon there together. The sun moves behind the mountain before Tomas puts things into his bag. We stretch and turn our faces to the last rays of sunshine. La Loca yawns.

"I haven't felt this peaceful in a very long time," she sighs. "It's another world up here, the real world somewhere far off down below."

"This is the real world," Tomas says. "My world. It's all I've ever known. I know what is going on far off, but I'm not a part of it."

"I have to," I say.

"Have to what?"

"Be a part of it. My father is in that world, my family, friends. I have to... well, I have to try to make a difference in some way."

"But how? What difference can you make with the *fascistas*? You have no power."

"I don't know yet, don't know what I'm going to do, but... there are different kinds of power, power that kills, destroys, and the kind that heals, convinces, transforms. I have to try."

La Loca has been silent. "I feel that. I know that if I do nothing, I'll die, just wither inside and die. The women, Angelita, they take all kinds of abuse, and not only verbal. They can't be educated, have property, can't vote or protest the injustices. If they do, they're thrown into prison and abused. I have to do something. There are protest groups and safe houses "

I turn to her, careful not to reach out physically. "Everything you say is true, I've heard from those who've been there, and not just Madrid, but all over Spain, in the villages, the towns and cities, also in the *campo*. There's even less protection for women there."

"Then you see why I have to go with you. We'll be stronger together."

"No. We won't. We will not be stronger together. Tomas has given me clothes to travel as a boy. It's the only way. The coast, Malaga, Almeria, all are unsafe, and I'd never get a train. I have to go overland. You couldn't, *amiga*. You could never fake it. You are woman all the way through. There are too many risks."

"I'm used to being unsafe!" she protests. "And I've survived!"

"I must go alone. There's no other way. You are to stay here with Tomas and his family and Maria del Mar. You must see that it's best for her." I have hit the right note, for she loves the child. She gazes at her in the water and is silent.

"Later, I'll send word, when things have settled down a bit and I have a safe place, then you can join me."

"Is that a promise?"

"It is. And I never break a promise," I tell her.

Tomas has listened in silence.

"It is best, my friend, not to argue, but to accept," he says quietly. "Angelita has always planned to go alone to Madrid. You have her word. She will send for you. And the child will stay here. You know the *Gitano* code. We take care of our own."

To my surprise and relief, La Loca nods. "I know. And I understand. I will stay. For now."

"Settled," Tomas nods, his face creased with concern. "I will go ahead of you now, and explain everything to my parents. I'll wave to you from the top when it's time for you to come up." Gathering up the food bag, he heads for the mountain.

It doesn't take long for the family to make us welcome. Tomas has three younger sisters, curious, lively, kind and playful with Maria del Mar. His mother and father quietly accept the situation as obvious and right.

"*Claro que si*," his mother says. "You must stay here, my children. We are not rich, but we are never short of food. You can help with the vegetables or in the orchard."

His father is a gruff, kindly man of few words who lets his wife make most of the decisions. "You can all help with the basket-weaving. We take them to local markets and to some places farther down." His children adore him.

The youngest girl climbs onto his lap, kisses his bearded cheek. "Just think, Papy, we'll have another sister, and I won't be the baby anymore." She jumps down, runs to Maria del Mar and hugs her. "I've got a doll," she says, "Mama made it for me." The two little girls hold hands and run off together.

The children are ecstatic when they discover that La Loca can dance.

"We want to learn!" the girls clamour.

La Loca grins twirls a little. " We'll start tomorrow." The girls clap and squeal their approval.

*

I stay for a week. Careful preparations are made for the journey to Madrid. Everything I will need for at least a week is stuffed into the leather rucksack Tomas has given me.

"Your other bag is too pretty," he insists. "No boy would carry that. And your hair. If you don't cut it, then tie it up in a bun on top, some boys do that. The really important thing is that the cap covers most of your face."

His father busies himself drying sausage and beef strips. "These will last forever and will give you the energy you'll need."

The main problem is water. There is only so much I can carry.

"Watch out for springs," he counsels. "Fill up whenever you have the chance. Remember, the Moors knew these mountains well before Ferdinand and Isabel drove them out, and they were clever. Water was sacred to them. You will learn to find their springs all over the place by feeling the ground and watching for damp rocks, the sign that water trickles through. And by seeing where the animals go to drink. Follow them."

As the day to leave approaches, Tomas and La Loca become very quiet. The sun has not yet risen behind the mountain. Dressed in the cap and jacket Tomas has given me, his rucksack on my back, I turn to say goodbye. They are nowhere to be seen. Puzzled and disappointed, I kiss the sleeping Maria del Mar and make my way down the hill. They stand at the pond, watching me.

"Take this with you," says Tomas, his voice low. He can't meet my eyes. "It belonged to my great grandmother. It is a talisman, for protection. Never let it go."

I glance down at the thing he has placed in my hand: a golden oval disc suspended from a thick golden chain. In the centre of the disc is engraved one word: *Libertad*. The ancient watch-word of the *Gitanos*, freedom.

"My great grandmother made it. There used to be gold in the rivers around here and in some there still is." He leans forward and kisses me on the mouth. He turns and walks away.

La Loca turns to me. "I have nothing to give you, only my love and loyalty. Forever." She puts her arms around me, this woman who cannot not bear to touch, and holds me in an embrace so rare, so gentle, I feel tears begin to spring.

Abruptly she turns and walks away towards the mountain.

I cannot watch them leave. I make my way to the forest below and am swallowed by the bleak darkness of the trees that seem to me like bitter sentinels watching my flight. For that is what it is, a leaving to an unknown place. Ice has formed upon the fallen leaves. I shiver, pull my cloak around me, shove my hands into my pockets. My fingers close around the golden disc. I take it out and press it to my lips. Words tumble into my head, words and sounds against the background of the tall dim whispering trees.

Take me into the hollow of your hand/where there is gentleness/light along the way as night turns into day/ and I recall the lowered lustre of your eyes/the pained disguise/the touch that fades/the sun and laughter of the days/the joy that lingers/the touch of your fingers on my hair/the peace of knowing/I'm surrounded/by your love/stay with me/the journey home is long/oh, hear my song...

I am startled by a sudden violent rustling beneath the trees, something surging from the brush. It is only an eagle owl. I watch its great wings beat skyward. As I walk, I sing. I do not look back.

four

I T IS THREE DAYS BEFORE I HAVE ANY HUMAN CONTACT.
I walk carefully, always alert to my surroundings. At the
end of the third day, I hear movement in the forest ahead,
creep carefully through the trees, and watch.

A group of about eight men are working on the trees,
cutting, stacking the wood into large piles. I creep back to
my hiding place in a dip behind the trees and take out my
blanket. It is cold in the forest. The trees are tall and thick
and obscure the warmth of the sun. I wrap myself in the
blanket and lie down. I think about what to do next. Nothing
for the moment, I decide. I will rest and sleep. Tomorrow I
will approach the men to see if I can join them, work with
them. I have no idea who they are, or where they come from,
but from their build and voices, it seems they are country
folk from surrounding areas, making a living from logging.
They will likely be Republicans in these mountains. But I
am not sure. I can only find that out by talking with them. I
have to be careful. My story about trying to reach my father
in Madrid is not so far from the truth. This will be the first
test of my disguise, and I am apprehensive. I have practiced,
rehearsed with Tomas's help the voice and movements of a
young boy. What if the men see through it? What if...

I will myself to calmness, whisper the lessons Tomas had

given me: when to speak, what about, how to lower my voice, how to show respect for my elders. That is important. I go over everything in my mind, and finally, as a sliver of moon appears between the trees, I fall asleep.

"What have we here!" a loud voice above me says.

I scramble to my feet, pulling the cap down, wiping the sleep from my eyes. Sideways before me stands a broad large man with orange hair, urinating against a tree.

"Don't be scared, lad," he laughs. "Not every day I find a boy in the woods when I'm taking a piss." He buttons his trousers and moves away. "If you're looking for work, come and see me after you wake up. We've got some coffee on."

Heart pounding, I button my jacket, glad I'd kept it on in the night. A sense of relief overwhelms me. I've passed the first hurdle. He thinks I'm a boy!

As soon as I get my shoes on, the thick mannish ones Tomas has given me, I make my way to the clearing. It is still early. The men are sitting around a small fire roasting sausages and drinking coffee. The big man gets up as I approach.

"Ah, there you are, lad. Sit down and warm up. You look like an icicle in a snowstorm. Here." He hands me a tin mug. "No sugar, too scarce."

The other men glance up and nod, busy with their food.

"We could use a nimble lad to shin up the trees and secure the chain," he continues. "Have any experience with that?"

I lower my voice as Tomas taught me. "No, but I'm a quick learner. And I need the work."

"Doesn't pay much, but you'll get your food and drink. How old are you?"

"Just eighteen."

"Small for eighteen," says one of the men. "But size isn't everything."

All the men laugh. "That's for sure," says one. "I've seen yours when you take a piss. Pity your poor wife."

I feel my face grow hot and will myself not to blush or stammer.

"Good things come in small packages," I quip. The big man roars with laughter and claps me on the shoulder. I manage to keep my feet.

"You'll do, lad." He grins. "We could do with a laugh around here. Make up for not having women for months at a time. When you've finished, join us over there by those trees, and I'll show you what to do. Right, men, to work!"

Clearly the big man is the boss of the group. His name is Antonio, but the men call him Fat Bastard with a certain tongue-in-cheek affection. He is strict but fair and well liked. The nickname suits his huge fleshy frame and broad shoulders and his direct, no holds barred approach to the men when he issues orders.

It doesn't take me long to learn the job he assigns to me. I go back to get my stuff in the woods and pull on an old pair of floppy trousers. Each man beds down by himself under a bivouac in case of rain in the night, easy to dismantle and move on when they need to. They assign me a niche in the corner of the bivouac. I fling my things down and get to work. I'm strong and nimble. As I work, they nod in approval.

Soon it becomes clear that they are not planning to spend all their time in the woods, logging. I overhear them talking and realize they are moving slowly towards Madrid, earning a living on the way in any way they can.

"There are problems there," I hear Fat Bastard say. "We have to get to the safe house within three weeks to join the Resistance."

I am relieved. They are Republicans eager to join the Resistance to Franco's regime. As time passes, I learn something about most of them. Nearly all have families and children, one left a pregnant wife with his father-in-law. Another, no older than seventeen, joined the Resistance after what happened to his sister in Malaga. He is a long way from home, downcast and almost childlike much of the time. But he works hard; they all do, and make their plans. All have a story to tell. They talk of the capture of women and children, their fear for their families, and their determination to bring about change.

Words start to form in my head.

Tomorrow, mujeres libres/do what you must/but be gentle/for perhaps tomorrow/ the children are coming/ the children are coming/bearing hopes held high/arms in the air/screaming as they run/throwing their fear into the wind/eyes raised to the morning/to a chance/ of arms that shelter/perhaps tomorrow.

I know I can never sing the songs to the men, for although my voice has a good range and I can sing low, it is a feminine voice. At night, I write the songs down in my notebook and tuck it into my rucksack. Later I will put the words to music, when I can practice unheard.

In the group is a young Irishman of about twenty-four, with roguish blue eyes and a ready grin, who has come to Spain to join the International Brigade and the Resistance.

His name is Seamus O'Brien and he studied Spanish in Edinburgh, Scotland. "I know what it's like to be under the heel of a tyrant," he tells the men. "The English have very sharp heels, and they like potatoes, but they don't care for the Irish!"

One day during rest time, he comes up to me.

"If you don't mind me sayin', young 'un, I'm on to your little secret," he says in a low voice so only I can hear. "I'm sure you've got your reasons, and I won't squeal. But you've got to stop squatting when you pee. No boy does that."

He sees my alarm and raises his hand to his lips. "Don't worry. I only saw you when I went a bit away from the camp for a rest, and there you were. But be careful." He smiles, turns and walks away.

I am careful to move farther from camp and into bushes from then on, grateful for the Irishman's confidence. Next time, I'm not so lucky.

*

The group has moved on to another area near a tiny village. Something happens that makes me realize how important it is to safeguard my disguise.

A young woman from nearby has come to take water from the stream and pauses to drink. One of the men, Romero, jumps forward to encircle her body from behind with both arms. I am about to move forward when she suddenly swings the bucket with all her might up and backwards towards his head. Cursing, he lets go of the girl and clutches his face. She slides away and dives into the stream, half stumbling, driven forward by the rushing water.

"Bitch! I'll get you for that!" Romero yells, running along the bank, clutching his bleeding nose. After a while the woman disappears from sight, and he gives up.

I retreat deeper into the woods where he can't see me and stand watching the *golondrinas* swooping in lace-like formation against the sunset, heading for Africa now that the weather has turned colder. There's a movement behind me. I turn to see Romero watching me.

"You must love that damn hat. You never take it off. Take it off, boy!" I back away. "You're a bit light for a lad your age. Eighteen, isn't it?"

I nod. Suddenly he reaches for the hat. I brush his arm away.

"Don't."

"Don't what?"

"Don't touch my hat. My father gave it to me."

"Ha! Sure it wasn't a girl?" He smirks. "Eh? Eh? Or don't you like girls?"

"My hat is sacred to me," I lie, ignoring the jibe. "My father gave it to me before he died."

Romero looks down, mumbles something, starts to turn away, and turns back suddenly. "Hey, you're not one o' them bum-fuckers, are you? Well, let's find out, beggars can't be choosers."

He grapples my hips from behind. I bring my elbow up with all my strength, backwards into his face. There's a crunch as I make contact with his nose. He lets go abruptly, clutching his face, blood pouring from his nose, and stumbles away, cursing. I hope his nose is broken. Romero glares at me. I make my way quickly back to camp.

Romero is not popular with the men. His breath stinks,

he is lazy and leaves as much work as he can get away with to the others while he sits around eating and brushing his limp greasy hair over a bald patch. I've heard them refer to him derisively as *maricon*, a jibe about his sexuality. They are suspicious about his attack on me and think he's gotten what he deserves. The men have heard the lie about my father and the hat, believe it, think I am grieving, respect that and are kindly, handing me extra food, pouring more coffee.

That night I think again about the hat incident and wonder if it is safe to rely on the bun tied up underneath the hat, or whether I should cut my hair.

A day before we reach the outskirts of Madrid, I decide to leave the group. Fat Bastard has got the men together to talk about their next movements. They are to enter the city from the west and head for where the Resistance has a safe house just inside the city suburbs. I know it is time to go my own way. I tell Fat Bastard privately that I have to go on alone, to find relatives. He understands.

"You've been a good lad," he says gruffly. "And you know the risks the Resistance is up against. Take care. You'll be missed."

Next day just before sunrise, I toss my few belongings and some food into the rucksack and make my way towards the city. It soon dawns on me that I have a monumental task before me. For the first time since leaving the pond, I feel truly alone. In this city, there is no kindness, no tolerance. People look anxious, cowed and watchful, like hungry dogs. The city reeks like a swamp, discarded garbage flung aside and left to rot, or scavenged by urchins. Guardia swagger about in twos or groups, sweating in the heat. Some of the privileged are visible through café windows, eating tapas and sipping wine. Children stop to gaze longingly at the feasting within, to be shooed away by a waiter at the doorway.

I slump onto a bench by a plaza and feel inside my rucksack for bits of cheese and bread. My hand encircles something long and firm. I pull it out. A huge sausage! My mouth waters at the smell of the meat. Fat Bastard must have shoved it there before our farewell at the outskirts of the city. Such kindness nobody would ever suspect from this rude, ungainly man.

Now I am lost. I have not the slightest idea where my father's house is. I would recognize the house, but the street, the area? I might as well have been in a maze. I come to a park with a tall open gate and enter. In the forgiving shade of a jacaranda tree, I sit down and pull out the sausage, ripping it open with my teeth, chewing blissfully. Soon I grow sleepy and lie down, my head on the rucksack, first removing my hat and placing it carefully under the rucksack.

I awake to silent darkness, sit up and look about. Not a soul in sight. I reach for the rucksack and my hand grasps at emptiness. Gone! I fight down a surge of panic and run to the gate. Locked! A dim glow from a faraway street lamp the only light. I glance back at the jacaranda tree. Something glistens on the ground, and as I grope about, my hand fastens on the hat, the silver emblem on its front twinkling in the distant light. I shove it on. I reach into my pocket for the golden disc Tomas gave me and press it to my lips. A chill strokes my spine at the memory of what I have left behind. I have never experienced being trapped. The wild freedom I have known all my life is far away, the space of valleys, the sheltering mountains and clear waters. I sink back onto the ground beneath the jacaranda tree.

Behind me, a movement.

"Is this what you are looking for, young lady?" a deep voice from behind the nearby tree says. A man emerges from the shadows. I cannot see his face, only a tall shadow. I back away, fumbling for my knife, only to realize it is in my rucksack, which dangles from his hands as he approaches.

"Not a good idea to fall asleep in this park," the voice says. "Too many *robbers*. I saw you sleeping and kept it for you."

"What do you want?" I demand, trying to still the shaking in my voice.

"To talk."

"Just to talk? Give me my rucksack!"

He tosses the rucksack towards me but does not move forward. "If you don't want to talk, that's fine. But it is a long night."

I relax slightly at the lack of aggression in his voice. There is a calmness about it, a confidence or authority, as though he is used to encountering people in the dark.

"How did you know?" I ask carefully

"How did I know what?"

"How did you know I was a girl? No-one has noticed that for months."

"It was hard to miss. Your hair was spread all over the rucksack, and your skin was soft."

I step back, alarmed now. "My skin? You *touched* me?" I grope about for something to protect myself with, a piece of wood, anything, and curse not having slept with the knife by me.

"I had to make sure," he replies matter-of-factly. "You didn't even move, and I let you sleep. You were exhausted."

What he says is hard to believe. I remember the warnings from Tomas. *Trust no man! Trust no-one. You are beautiful and young. Men will want to touch you, to own you.* Here is a man who has touched me, and I am still free and rested. And scared. I realize I will have to try to humour him, until it is light. Then surely the gate will be unlocked and I can leave.

"You must be thirsty. There are no crystal streams here, but I have some water." He rolls a flask towards me but does not step forward. Cautiously, I pick up the flask and drink greedily, one eye on the dark shape by the tree.

Silence.

"Why do you speak of crystal streams? You know nothing about me! Why are you doing this? What do you want from me? I demand to know!" I shout with a courage I do not feel, born of desperation and fear. I am not used to feeling helpless.

"It's the way you speak. You're a mountain girl and a long way from home, I think. And I thought you needed help."

"I do. I need to get out of here. The gates are locked."

"I have a key."

"What!"

"I have a key," he repeats calmly.

"Then let me out."

"Of course. But where will you go? It is not safe. It is better to stay here until dawn breaks."

"I don't believe you have a key! And anyway, why should you care!"

The man walks slowly to the gate, unlocks it, and stands aside. In the gloom, I see that he is tall, broad-shouldered, and standing up straight. He holds the gate open. I do not move.

"Good decision," he says, closes and locks the gate and walks back to his tree, careful to avoid me.

"Why do you have a key?"

"Part of my job."

"Your job? You are a park keeper?"

"I work for the government."

"You… you work for… the fascists? For the bastard who murders his own people?"

"I am a soldier."

"You're a fascist! You work for the tyrant!" In my outrage, I feel no fear.

Silence.

I make no effort to hide my disgust. "You have no answer."

There is a stirring by the tree, as if he is about to make a decision. I finger the knife in the rucksack. The man does not move.

"I have a child," he says, "a small daughter. Her mother is dead…"

"And that's your justification?"

"It is… it is an explanation," he says quietly. "I will not risk the life of my child. That's why I work for the government. You… you reminded me of her as you slept. That's why I locked the gate and removed your rucksack. It is not safe here."

Footsteps echo in the streets beyond the gates, and light is moving behind the tall buildings lining the park. Shapes of people creep towards the gates.

"I suppose you like to be seen as a warrior, but you don't understand what you are fighting for. You strike out blindly."

Silence at first. Then, "I am no warrior. I am a father," he says quietly.

"How can you live with yourself? It's every man for himself here! And the women... the women don't stand a chance, no rights, no education, no freedom... and you—"

"I know this."

"You with a daughter! How do you think she will survive her future? How she will fulfill her dreams—"

"Sit, please," he says suddenly, "until light comes, then I will unlock the gate."

I sit, feeling that I've lost control of the moment. Intuition tells me I am safe, but I am watchful, Tomas's clear voice still in my head: *trust no-one.*

"You are right to trust no-one," the man says, as if he has read my mind.

Wind shakes the branches. The sheltering tree weaves and creaks above me. It feels like an omen of things to come. I stand up.

"Let me out."

"I will open the gate," he says, and pauses. "Where are you headed?"

"To my father. He is frail and he needs me. Open the gate."

"You know where he lives, of course. The zone."

I hesitate. *Never reveal too much. They will use it against you.* But I do not know the zone. "I know only the name of the street and the house."

"Well, that's a start, but it's a big city. You have to know the zone. I could help you find it."

"I have told you I don't know it."

"Then you have a problem."

I've been holding my breath and release it in a gust of

frustration. "I'm sure I'll manage," I say, and move towards the gate.

"I think I can help you. With the zone, I mean. But I'd have to call on someone first for the information you need. And the name."

"Name?"

"Your father's name. To match the address."

I hesitate, uncertain about giving my father's name to this stranger. Swiftly I weigh the alternative: I will never find my father's house in this maze of a city.

"De Caballe," I say finally. "Bruno de Caballe. He…"

"Bruno de Caballe!" the man exclaims. "He is well known. He was a captain." He moves toward the gates.

"I'll wait here," I say and sit.

"All right, but… put that cap back on, and tie up your hair underneath. When I leave, stand here in my place. It is quite well hidden. I'll be back when I have the information."

I watch him leave, moving easily and swiftly. Remembering his warning, I tuck my hair up under the cap, grab the rucksack, move back behind his tree, and wait.

A few minutes later, I hear movement near the clearing I have just left. Two men are talking, making no effort to hide or talk quietly, thinking themselves alone. They flop down in the place I have just left. I realize with relief that they are unaware of my presence behind the tree.

"If we wait long enough, someone will come and unlock the gate," says one.

"Then, they sweep the park for escapees and Republicans."

"Maybe there's some girls hiding," says the first. "I'd like that. Could do with a good fuck. It's been a long time."

"Me too!" grunts the other. "For now, I'll just have to rely on my hand."

I shudder and wonder when the tall man will return. I have no alternative but to trust him, especially now. I am hungry and thirsty but dare not move nor make a sound. These men are rough, desperate. For some time, I have passed as a boy but have no way of knowing how long the subterfuge will last. Especially in the hostility and cynicism of this city. I pull back behind the tree and press my face against the bark, my legs rigid with tension, too afraid to sit. I think about my father. He is well known; indeed, a legend. Believed dead in a landslide in the rain-soaked mountains of Cantabria while on a mission, he survived. All his men perished, sucked into the muddy valley below. How he had survived was a mystery to most. He told me the story.

He and his men were returning from quelling a Resistance near the border with France and took shelter from torrential rain in a hillside cave. They were there for five days, starving, freezing, trapped. When the rain stopped suddenly, he took his men across a narrow ledge that led to the valley below. But the ledge crumbled. There was no way back. They could see the valley below and this gave them courage to edge forward. But torrential rain began again. A giant slug of mud slid over the men and sucked them into the chasm below. My father was in front, balanced precariously on a narrow shelf of rock, when the wall behind him collapsed and he fell backwards into darkness, hit his head on a rock and passed out. He had fallen into a long, narrow cave under the hills with a small opening into a pasture beyond. He survived by clutching the legs of a passing mountain goat, gorged on the flesh and drank the blood. Eventually, he managed to squeeze through the opening into a meadow. He caught and ate rabbits, herbs and wild asparagus. In time, he made his way down the mountain to the valley, dry in the spring sunshine. He remembered nothing of the past for a year. When his memory returned, with it came an embittering rage and a longing for his past life, the image of my mother and his love for her always in his thoughts, driving him forward.

These memories, the stories of his struggles, fill me with pity. Now he is old, and alone in this city. I will find him.

Time drags on and still no sign of the tall man. Fingers of light spread behind the buildings, movement increases to a sluggish shuffling, and with a feeling of rising panic, I wonder if I've made the right decision to trust this man.

I hear a fumbling at the gate and the scrape of a key in the lock. The tall man enters, closes the gate without locking it, walks towards me. The two men get to their feet and stand silently, waiting. Should I call out, warn him? To my relief, the two men walk quickly past him to the gate, open it, and leave.

"What's wrong?" the tall man asks. "You look shaken."

"I thought you weren't coming back… I don't even know your name… I was afraid… it was growing light… those two men…"

"I am Joaquin. I should have told you before I left. Those men are thugs, thieves and… I'm glad I came when I did." He places his arm gently around my shoulders. "I have the information you need. But first, breakfast."

We go to a nearby café. I wolf down the eggs and bread hungrily and sip the hot coffee.

"Now I'll take you to your father's house. I have a car nearby." He sees my hesitation. "If I'd wanted to harm you, I could have done so. I do not. Let's go."

After some time, as we drive through the city, I recognize the area: the plaza, a café close by, and the street.

"Here," I say. "Let me out here."

"I'll wait until you are sure and until you enter the house."

I am sure. I grab my rucksack and get out of the car.

"Wait." Joaquin reaches into his pocket, tears a page from a notebook and writes something down. "My telephone number. Call me if you need anything." He watches me walk to the door and fit the key my father gave me into the lock. The door opens. He drives away.

five

SUNLIGHT FLASHES ON THE SILVER SURFACE OF THE key, and for a moment, I am blinded. I stand very still and listen. Silence. I push the heavy studded door open and enter. A board creaks as I make my way along the shadowy hall. I stop and wait, listening. No movement, the only sounds the distant shriek of an ambulance racing up the avenue, a screech of tyres, the yelp of a dog. My father is probably still asleep. But the bedroom is empty. There is a reek of stale urine from the open bathroom door.

I push open the study door. He sits at the great mahogany desk, a tall stack of papers beside him. One by one he crumples them and tosses them into a metal bin. The papers whisper on the metal as they fall. Gently I close the door, make my way back down the hall to the salon and sit down to wait until he is ready.

On a table by the window is a stack of papers. I reach idly for one of the papers and read. It appears to be my father's memoir or autobiography. I read on in horror and disbelief, one page after the other until I can read no more. I stare unseeingly out at the street, palpitations in my chest, my mouth dry, remembering.

I was sixteen at the time, reading the books in my father's library in Madrid. I read one about twelve women executed for supporting their Republican men and took it to share with my father. His rage terrified me. He grabbed the book, threw it on the fire and stormed from the room.

Now I understand. He explains why in graphic detail in the notes in front of me.

Stunned, trembling, I replace the papers on the table, grab my rucksack and let myself quietly out of the front door.

Outside, I wonder what to do, where to go. I recognize the area and move towards the main square. A narrow street leads from the square to a small café I know. I enter, sit down, and order coffee. My mind is in turmoil. I know I cannot go back to the house. Perhaps I will never return. Yet there will have to be a reckoning, a confrontation, a confession, or whatever it is that happens between two people who have loved and been betrayed. I do love my father. All the years of tenderness and affection cannot be discarded like an old piece of clothing. I remember my brother's words. *One day, darling, when you are older, you will understand everything.* Well, I am older now. Really, I feel ancient and exhausted. I understand everything. My father's inexplicable rage years ago becomes painfully clear. I am certain only of one thing: what is revealed in those papers is unforgivable. But I hear my grandmother's voice whispering in my head. *To forgive is powerful. To withhold forgiveness is another kind of power.*

I lower my head onto my arms, heart racing. I force myself to breathe deeply.

"Are you all right, *senorita*?" The young waiter stands beside me, coffee in hand.

I sit back. "Just tired. *Gracias.*"

He puts down the cup. "Extra sugar. Good for energy."

I stare blindly into the street, the coffee untouched. Tears of fury and regret spring to my eyes. I pick up my pen and begin to write.

Blood of youth/paid for with arms that strike the heart/for the crime of loving/too deeply/those who stood in mud/and sang walking in darkness/Hold, sisters, hold!/Cry only for the blood of youth/the bonds of tyranny./For a moment courage fails/a howl of fear brings sisters close/touching as they fall/lives ebbing/ rubies on the sand.

I call the song "Twelve Roses."

I am unaware of the stares of other customers or of any movement around me. The young waiter places more coffee before me. I write until my hand hurts. I place the pen on the table, shake the blood back into my fingers, pick the pen up and go on writing. Notes of another song ring in my head, low dark sounds, rising… not one voice but many voices, singing. A chorus.

This morning, with the early sun slicing blade-like through the shutters, "The Cemetery of Forgotten Women" is born. I cannot know then how prophetic the words will be and how I will come to know their true meaning.

I rummage in my rucksack for the telephone number Joaquin gave me and call to the waiter that I need to use the telephone and will pay him. He beckons me to a small room, and I go inside to make the call.

A voice answers that I do not recognize.

"Captain Montenegro, please."

"One moment. Hold."

I wait for what seems an eternity. Then the familiar, deep voice.

"Montenegro here."

"Joaquin, it's me."

"Angelita! I didn't expect to hear from you so soon."

I swallow. "I didn't expect to call so soon."

"Your voice sounds strange…"

"I can't go back to my father's house…"

"What is it? Where are you?"

"Café Placita, near the main square."

"I'll be there in two hours. I must finish up here first."

"I'll wait."

I go back to the table, glad I've taken the rucksack with me. The café is filling up with people ordering café and cognac and tostadas.

Joaquin arrives an hour and a half later, face creased with concern. He sits opposite me, searches my face, waits for me to speak. After five minutes, I have still said nothing.

"What has happened? Is it… is your father all right?"

I look bleakly at him. "He didn't expect me."

"I know, you told me that, but surely he was pleased to see you."

"He didn't see me."

"I don't understand."

"I left before he could see me."

"But… why? Why, after coming all this way?"

"I went in quietly so as not to wake him. He was up already. He was in his office, writing. I went back to the salon to wait for him." My pulse hammers in my head.

"Here, drink this." He pushes a glass of water towards me.

"Take your time."

I gulp the water. "There was a stack of papers on the table, a kind of memoir, an account of his activities when he was active in the government, his job of… of forcing confessions, the incarcerations, torture…"

He takes my arm and steers me to the door. I lean on him the short distance to the car, tumble inside and fling my head back on the seat, sobbing.

He waits in silence. I cry until an empty dryness clutches my stomach. I turn to look at Joaquin. His face is tight with concern, but he doesn't speak. He takes a notebook from his pocket and writes something down.

"I don't know what to do," I say.

"Nothing. Do nothing, for now. You can't go back there. You can stay at my house with Estella and me until you've recovered and decided what to do. The maid comes daily, but that's not a problem. We can go there now. Then I have to get back."

I feel some pressure lift off me.

"In time," he says slowly, "there are things I have to tell you about myself, my own life. But not now. I think you have enough to deal with for the moment. We'll go to my house now."

The house is about a half-hour drive away, on a leafy street of trees and two-story stone houses. A small iron gate encloses a garden of roses encircling a patch of grass. I inhale the scent of the flowers and touch the soft petals. I think of the "Twelve Roses" and a sob rises in my throat.

"There are more in the back," Joaquin says. He opens the blue wooden door and stands aside. I enter a broad hallway brightly painted in blue and orange, light filtering from a large window at the far end. He shows me the salon, a spacious light-filled room with two large sofas, a piano at one end, and a door opening onto a long narrow garden obscured from neighbouring houses by tall trees.

"Your room is upstairs," he said. "It used to be my daughter's, but she's next to it now. Come, I'll show you."

The room is small and overlooks the garden, a quilted bed on one side, on the other a chair and desk. I place my rucksack on the floor and sit on the bed.

"The bathroom is just past Estella's room on the right. She'll be back later. Isabel picks her up after school. There are towels there. I'll be back this evening." He turns away towards the stairs.

"I won't forget this," I call. He waves a hand in a soldierly salute.

I flop onto the bed and stretch my legs, curl into the pillow and fall asleep. It is still light when I awake, the sun slightly lower behind the trees in the long garden below. I have fallen asleep without covering myself and feel chilled. I walk down the hall to the bathroom and run hot water into the bath. In the bedroom, I lay out clean clothes from my rucksack and gaze out into the garden lined with yellow blossoms framing a green lawn. I stretch, inhale the fresh air deeply into my lungs, and will myself to put aside the events of the morning.

I sink into the bath and let the warmth caress me, plunge my head under the water to wash the sweat and grime of the long journey from my hair, wrap myself in one of the big blue towels, sit down at the desk in the little room and take up my pen. The words have a life of their own. They pour onto the pages, tumbling over each other. I can hardly write fast enough. Something takes shape; a song forms, sounds in my head. Everything in my young life, all the things I have done, the adventures, the living, violence and loving, all of these have led up to this moment. This is what I was born to do: to listen, watch, feel, to take this gift I have been given and transform all of it into song. For the first time, I know I truly understand in my heart what it is I have to give, why I cannot be caged, a songbird without flight.

I dry myself and dress in the fresh clothes, make my way downstairs to the salon and cross to the piano. I pick out notes, humming. As I play, I hear many voices of women in my head raised in protest and longing and pain, sometimes in chorus, sometimes alone.

In the hall, a child's voice, high and joyful. Estella runs into the salon, hugs me and makes straight for the piano. Oblivious to Isabel and her father and me, she goes on playing and doesn't notice that we've left the room. Isabel prepares *almuerzo,* main meal of the day. Vegetables, nuts, salad, chicken, all go onto the round table by the window; wine and water, and a bowl of oranges for dessert. Isabel leaves to be with her family, who live nearby.

Joaquin pours two glasses of Rioja, hands one to me.

"She'll be in there playing for a while," he says, "so you have time to enjoy this and relax."

"She's lovely. That fair hair," I say. "I see why I reminded you of her in the park. The same colour hair."

Estella is beautiful. Large soft brown eyes in an oval face, an impetuous impish grin, perfect small limbs that will grow into full bloom one day. She has no reserve, no shyness, perhaps because she is in her own home with her father and her beloved piano.

"She's gifted," I say.

"She is. And she makes up all these notes on her own. She had a music teacher who taught her to read, but the teacher was very traditional, lots of scales and repetition, and Estella finally asked to give her up. She can read music but says she prefers to listen and play by ear."

"What does she listen to?"

"Just things she hears on the radio or in the parks and streets. Sometimes she plays things I've never heard of. I ask her how she hears them, and she says she just hears things all the time, sounds and rhythms, even when she's just walking down the street. Sometimes she stops and listens. Then she comes back and starts playing notes on the piano."

He refills my glass and goes into the hall to call his daughter to eat.

Joaquin is often absent on missions involving his work as a captain. After I have been there a week, he tells me things about himself that make me uneasy. He works undercover for the Resistance. It is risky. The subterfuge can be exposed at any time by a minor error, a wrong decision. This is a risk he is prepared to take. The murder of his wife by the fascists has convinced him that they must be stopped. But not at all costs.

"I have two good reasons for keeping my position: the ability it provides me to secretly undermine and oppose the regime; but most of all, to protect my daughter. I modify all my decisions according to her needs."

Estella is the guiding star in his universe, leading him on an uncertain and uneven course. He has made arrangements for her safety in the event of his arrest. His maid Isabel knows and is part of those arrangements.

As the days pass into weeks, the weeks into months, Joaquin and I become close. There is nothing we cannot talk about, nothing we cannot share. We have to be careful, but Isabel is no risk. She lost her husband to the Guardia in Catalunya and has no idea where he is or even if he is still alive. They took him in the middle of the night while they were asleep, breaking down the door, leaving without explanation. That was a year ago. Since then, she has moved to his sister's house in Madrid. She has no children of her own and loves Estella like a daughter.

Isabel and I become friends, a feminine understanding and empathy. When I play and sing "Twelve Roses," I turn to find her standing by the door silently listening, tears pouring down her cheeks. I cross to the door and lead her to the sofa. She sits, sobbing.

"One of them was my kid sister," she says at last. "Her husband was caught too."

I put my arms around her and lay her head upon my shoulder. We sit like that for some time, not speaking. Joaquin appears at the door, nods, and leaves quietly to make lunch.

We have a lot in common, Joaquin and I. We love nature, music, and children. But most of all, we are united in our hatred of the government and a conviction that we must work for change. I outline my plans to him for music, dance and protests.

"You will never be allowed to perform in public, in theatres or concert halls," he says. "That's forbidden and strictly enforced, unless the government approves performances, of course."

I have heard about this. "That means my performances, of course. Anything I do would never be approved."

"Never." He pauses. "But... there are other ways, risky ways. That's where I can help."

I am excited, curious. "How? I need to know."

What he tells me changes my life.

six

THE DAYS AT JOAQUIN'S HOUSE PASS AS IN A DREAM, music drifting from the salon, a scent of flowers from the garden. The ache inside me is real, a physical pain. The conflicting emotions I feel about my father subside into a dull, constant, anguished longing. I am unaware of the passage of time, carried along by a stream flowing to an unknown destination, sometimes crystal clear, often opaque and muddied. Some of the songs I share with Estella, the merry or jubilant ones, but they are few. I leave out those that express mature and terrifying experiences beyond the innocence of her own loved and sheltered life. Yet her compassion for the lost and hungry is deep in one so young.

One day, I join her while she plays. The notes are slow, mournful. When she turns to me, her eyes brim with tears. I put my arm around her.

"Estella, what is it?" I whisper.

"I was walking through the park," she sobs. "There was a man beating a dog. He went on beating it until it couldn't move. I think its leg was broken. I shouted at him, but he didn't stop. I ran all the way home to find Isabel, but she wasn't here."

"You must always come to me," I say, kissing her forehead. "I'm usually upstairs or in the garden. What you saw was horrible, cruel. There is so much... so much in the world that is unfair."

"And did you know that there are children without food? I saw some of them when I was walking with Papy in the central square. They were begging or picking bits of food from the bins. I gave one my apple, and he ran off with it. The others chased him."

"And what did you do when you came home?" I ask, knowing the answer,

"I ran straight to the piano and put a song there. Next, I'll put the words."

"Do you have the words already?"

"Some of them. The others are still in my head."

"That's why you were crying."

She puts her small arms around me and holds tight. "I hope you stay with us always, Angelita," she murmurs.

My heart aches for the child. I see myself in her as a little girl, making up songs and singing them to the sky. My childhood has been less privileged in some ways, yet more liberated, suffering and trauma unknown to me until I reached pubescence and an awareness of the world outside my own sheltered existence. In my childhood, there was freedom, but also unspoken fears, unanswered questions leading me to explore and ultimately to rebel.

As time passes, my friendship with Joaquin deepens. I'd find him looking at me affectionately, his brown eyes bright with worry. When I tell him about my father, he simply holds me against his shoulder. As the days pass, I long for him to hold me again, to feel his strength, the warmth of safety. But he keeps his distance. It is as if he is waiting for something.

Perhaps he is waiting for a signal from me, a change in my feelings? I know that he cares for me, and I am puzzled. My only experiences with men have been the attack by the guard in the holding house, and later, Tomas's soft sweet loving by the pond. Those two experiences are so different from each other, so opposite in feeling and sensation: one full of terror and desperation, the other deep tenderness and touching that filled my whole being with a quivering wonder, like the fluttering of a butterfly's wings.

As the days turn into weeks, the weeks to months, I feel a growing need to be close to Joaquin. I stand beside him as he prepares lunch, letting my body touch his as I reach for something. There are vibrations between us, warmth in his responses to my touch. Sometimes he turns to smile at me. But still, he keeps his distance.

At night, I imagine I can hear him breathing, and visualize how he would look while sleeping and what it would be like to nestle close to him.

When he is free, the three of us walk to the parks together the child skipping happily between us. Her special treat is *churros con chocolate*, long crisp doughnuts dipped into thick, hot chocolate. Once as we sit enjoying these, Joaquin glances out of the window and tenses suddenly.

"Excuse me please, for a moment," he says. I watch him cross the street to talk with a man on the other side. Their interaction is swift and tense. Joaquin glances about and passes something to the man, who walks quickly away. I say nothing when Joaquin returns.

That night, after Estella has gone to bed, we sit opposite each other in the kitchen, sipping the Rioja left over from dinner.

"You are preoccupied," he observes.

"I've been thinking about the man you were talking to today."

He doesn't reply. I wait. He gazes out at the garden, looks down at his hands, begins to speak, and stops. "There are things about my life," he says at last, without looking at me. "Things you need to know about me. I think this is the time."

"Go on."

"I'm not who you think I am. I have not been that person for some time." He stops, looks at last into my eyes as he speaks. "I am working for the Resistance."

I have not expected this. I stare at him. "Go on," I say quietly.

The words pour out then like the unstoppable surge of a broken dam.

"My wife was from Barcelona. She was secretly involved in the Resistance. She was apprehended by one of Franco's men, passing information about a meeting to another woman. There was no trial. She was thrown into prison, tortured and executed. She had been working under an assumed name, and they never connected her to me. They never knew my wife. They thought she had abandoned Estella and me shortly after the birth and fled to England. They never discovered the truth. I am able to care for Estella and continue working. But not only for the government. From the day my wife was killed, I vowed to undermine and oppose them in any way I can. But as a spy for the Resistance, I have to be careful. I have Estella to protect. My rank and responsibilities allow me to do things, access information and plans that I could never otherwise obtain. It's risky, but it's the only way. The only way I can do something to bring down this brutal regime without endangering my daughter."

I stare at him in silence for a long time. He looks down at his hands, looks away. I cross to him, take his face gently between my hands, and kiss him on the mouth.

He rises and takes me in his arms.

"I had no idea how you would react—"

"Like this," I whisper and curl my arms around his neck.

Loving Joaquin is like reaching for the sky and finding a galaxy of blinding light. The journey of discovery stretches before us into the night and far beyond, an exploration of unimagined release and joy, enigmatic landscapes then unknown to us that we will one day have to confront.

*

My life in Madrid takes on a very different pace and colour than I expected. I feel a sense of growth from the music welling inside me. Nights are filled with the calm, deep fullness of being loved, sweet as molten honey on the tongue, my breasts swollen, my body vibrant with longing and ease.

I think of my father often. Reading his papers has left in me a residue of puzzlement and pain that I am not ready to confront. Everything I have ever believed of him, all I have known and cherished during my childhood—the warmth, gentleness and care—have been thrown into doubt and confusion.

Joaquin is often absent from home. His revelation that he is counteractive for the Resistance fills me with awe and dread. His subterfuge can be exposed at any time by a minor error in judgment, a wrong decision. This is a risk he is prepared to take. The murder of his wife planted a deep revulsion for the fascists in his soul and a conviction that they must be stopped.

*

As the months pass, I work on the songs and realize that the only gift I have to give is the one I have been born with: my voice. I do know how to shoot, how to defend myself, but I am not a *guerrera, a warrior* trained to kill and give my life for the cause. I am gripped by a passion more powerful than any gun or knife: the longing for justice and freedom from the despair consuming the people of my country, especially the women. I know the enemy. The government is like a tree ripe with fruit rotten at the core and ready to fall. I will shake that tree. I will kill the enemy softly with song and movement, poetry and the allegiance of good people. I will speak to the hearts of the just still left among us, the powerful in the government who still care for freedom.

"I have many contacts, I know where there are Resistance meetings in safe places, places outside the city with clear exit routes in the event of danger," Joaquin tells me.

"I need to know more. If it's safe for meetings, then why not for other things, for performances? I've heard of such places."

"They gather in safe houses, in cemeteries, old warehouses, sometimes in parks, even in abandoned morgues."

"But has it worked? There's no use preaching to the converted. We have to target people near the top, people who can bring about real change."

"I know. As I said, there are risks, mainly with those invited to the gatherings. We have to be careful. That's where I come in. I know many people in government who are unhappy with what's going on and want change but don't know how to go about it, how to unite. Some have lost friends, even family. They feel trapped. I have to be sure of them, and that takes patience and caution."

"But how do you find out if they are safe and can be trusted?"

"I do my research. I put in trusted 'workmen' to their homes to plant devices, I monitor conversations. That's how I find out what they really think. Then, if the time is right, I approach them. Cautiously. Deviously. My work as a captain at headquarters makes this possible."

"But the risks, to you, to Estella—"

"That's where I draw the line. I do nothing—nothing at all—that could endanger her."

"Yet if something were to happen unexpectedly—"

"I've thought of that. If we are discovered, there is a plan of action, an escape route. Isabel knows of it. You can trust her."

"Ah. I see." Our eyes meet. "Then we need to get to work." He nods.

I am anxious about such a course of action. But I am driven to producing more work. I plan, organize, look for possibilities.

As I work, I hear the rhythms in my head, the pulse and movement of La Loca dancing. I think of her often over the weeks that follow. Her special gift has a place in what I plan to do. The only way I can contact her is through Tomas. There is a *correos*, a mail office, in a pueblo two hours' journey from the mountains that is open for one hour each day. I can write to him there. I know that any communication, carries the risk of discovery, but it is the only way. There are no telephones in the mountains. Joaquin mails the letter that same day at the central office to be sure it goes out. The letter is short and to the point, asking that La Loca come to Madrid as soon as possible. I give the address and zone of the house.

I do not expect a reply for some time. Things move slowly in the valleys and mountains, Sometimes, if the weather is bad, the roads treacherous, the *carteros* do not bother to deliver mail at all, or toss it down the mountain.

I have no idea if or how La Loca will get to Madrid, but she is resourceful.

I hear Estella on the piano below. I go down to sit beside her and sing.

*

The sun slices across the table as I work on a song. I go down to the piano to pick out some notes. Nothing happens. I gaze out at the garden, seeing nothing, hearing in my head the sound of many voices, the voices of women speaking, screaming, crying out, singing. My single voice fades into the background, and I know what I have to do. This is, a protest not for one voice, but for many voices. A chorus of voices. The story has been in my dreams and nightmares and waking hours for a long time, since I first heard of the captured women in an elegant guarded place reserved only for the generals.

Joaquin looks for a place that will safely hold many people. I play the song to him. He is excited.

"It has movement, this song," he says. "Passion. It's as if the women should be moving as they sing. It's a powerful message, needs to be fluid, to move, maybe outwards among the watchers."

A vision of La Loca comes before me as he speaks. She must be part of this! Her gift of using her body through dance as an expression of her passion is needed here.

I think about the letter I've sent and wonder how long it will take, whether it will ever reach Tomas. It could be intercepted. What if La Loca has seen the letter and left without thought or preparation? She is impulsive. A woman of her beauty and sensuality will be noticed travelling alone. I try to push my misgivings aside and concentrate on the work.

Joaquin carefully explores possibilities for a venue and researches a way to involve the secret dissenters in the government. It is risky. Dangerous. He tells me to be vigilant, to monitor who comes to the house or lingers nearby. If the project is to succeed, time and caution are essential.

Two weeks after my revelation about the chorus, I sit at work, thinking and writing. There is a knock on the door. I freeze. Estella is at school, and Isabel isn't here yet. Afraid to make a sound, I sit in silence, listening. I become aware of a presence behind the door and resolve not to open it.

I hear a strange yet familiar sound on the other side of the thick wooden door, the sound of a dog or some other animal. It begins slowly, cautiously, and rises to a controlled pitch, a soft howling. I leap to my feet. *Could it... could it be...*

Softly, I repeat the sound. It is answered with a quiet, ascending howl, a wolf-call, increasing in intensity to a carefully controlled pitch. All caution gone, I rush to the door and fling it open.

"Tomas!" Behind him stands La Loca, exhausted, smiling. I throw the door wide and pull them quickly inside.

"How?" I cry, sobbing with relief and joy. We cling

together, blending as one body. In the kitchen, we stand gazing at each other, speechless with happiness.

"You must be hungry," I say. "I'll get some food, then you can tell me all about it."

"About what?" says La Loca, blunt as always. "We left, we travelled, now we're here."

Tomas grins. "We got your letter. I've been going to the *correos* every week just in case. We left as soon as we could. We posed as mother and son…"

"Pushing it a bit," interrupts La Loca. "I'd have had him at age ten!"

"It worked, though," Tomas laughs. "We got a wagon to Jaen, a bus from there to Ciudad Real. I had some money and paid for them. I made La Loca look older, downtrodden, loose dull clothing. We ran into some trouble at Ciudad Real, but La Loca danced and they let us go on."

"I stink," La Loca says. "Any chance of a bath?"

I take her up to the bathroom and run the water.

"You've a little paradise here," she sighs, looking about admiringly. "How on earth…?"

"Long story," I said. "Later. Go on, get in. You can use that blue towel."

Downstairs, Tomas has moved to the salon and is gazing out at the riotous pink and orange blossoms, luminous in the early morning sunshine. He turns as I come in.

"Dear Tomas. I've thought of you so often over these months."

"Me too, *carino*." He moves to take me in his arms but stops.

I come close to him and place my hand on his chest. "There's something I must tell you, dear friend."

"I know," he says quietly. "You are in love. It's written all over you, your eyes, the way you move." I am silent. "Is this his house?"

"It is. He found me when I was lost in the city park at night and helped me. He has a small daughter."

"He is married?"

"His wife was murdered by the *fascistas* in Barcelona. That's where she was from. She was visiting family and working for the Resistance when they caught her."

"And the man, her husband?"

"Joaquin. He's a captain in the First Division."

"*What?*"

"Listen. Just listen, Tomas. *Please!*"

"But, Angelita—"

"He is helping us—"

"Helping! Everything you've planned for could be put in jeopardy, could be at risk!"

I try to reassure him. "We can trust him, Tomas. Not just because of his wife, but because of his little daughter. He would never do anything to put her at risk."

"He has nothing to lose. You do." He takes my hand, kisses it. "I love you, Angelita. I can't pretend I'm happy with your news. I care that you're safe, happy, and…" He stops. Tears sparkle and he turns away. "I have something to show you."

I become alarmed as he removes his trousers, then his shirt. I stare, horrified. His whole body from neck to toe is covered in a mass of jagged, burned scars and fissures.

"This," he says, "is what can happen when you trust the wrong person."

seven

I SIT WITH TOMAS IN THE SHELTERING GREEN SHADE OF the long narrow garden. Tall trees on either side obscure us from the view of neighbouring houses. The sun slices through thick leaves and forms white daggers upon the grass in the early morning light. We inhale the scent of roses and savour the languid peace of the moment. There will be few such moments in the coming months.

"Tell me how Maria del Mar is and if she is happy."

"She loves being with my family and wants to stay there. She sends her love and hopes that you come back soon to the mountains."

Gently, I take Tomas's hand. "How did it happen?"

"I picked up your letter. Out in the street, I saw three Guardia approaching the *correos*. I know this happens sometimes but was willing to take the risk of mail being intercepted or destroyed and never reaching its destination. I couldn't risk revealing your address. I took a match and set fire to your letter just before the Guardia came through the door. They saw the ashes on the floor. First, they questioned me about the information in the letter. I refused. They took me outside to an abandoned field behind the main street and tied me to a fence post.

"'You like to play with fire,' the leader said. 'Get used to it. It gets a bit hot, but soon you'll feel nothing.'

"They placed straw all around me. They set fire to it and left, laughing. If it hadn't been for two neighbours who rushed out and smothered me with blankets, I'd be dead."

"Oh, Tomas, *carino*, you must be in such pain. We must get you to a doctor."

"No! I can't risk that. They'd want me to explain. They'd want to know where I'm staying, how it happened, how I found you. No. It would put all of us at risk, everything we planned would be in jeopardy."

"But, Tomas," I persist, "these wounds can be infected. It's dangerous. I can find someone who'll come to the house, someone we can trust. Joaquin will help us."

He shakes his head. "It's too risky."

"You're in no condition to move on, Tomas. These wounds will get worse if they're not treated. Then what? You could become very ill. Or die. And everything would be jeopardized anyway."

No answer. At first, I think his silence is assent.

"I can leave," he says at last. "Just disappear. Then you and La Loca can move on."

"Not an option," I tell him bluntly. "We will never move on without you. Do you understand? Never."

La Loca comes in and sits beside us. "You're a stubborn bastard, Tomas. I'm telling you, we will find someone to come here to the house. *Entendido?*"

Tomas, wincing, puts his arms around both of our shoulders. "Understood. I see I have no choice," he murmurs. "And I'm glad of that."

Through one of his trusted contacts, Joaquin finds a doctor who will come to the house. The doctor has been briefed on the problem and brings ointments and treatments to prevent infection of Tomas's wounds.

"Looks like you've been in a bit of a hot spot," is the doctor's wry comment. "You must administer these liniments rigorously for at least three weeks to avoid serious infection. If you bathe, do so in lukewarm water laced with olive oil. Avoid strenuous activity, unnecessary travel—and certainly not on horseback, for now."

Tomas bows slightly. "Thank you. I will pay you for the—"

"No payment," the doctor interrupts. "It's the least I can do for the cause." He moves to the door. "If you have no relief within two weeks, I shall return." He pauses and turns to me. "These are dangerous times," he says quietly. "Be vigilant, you have a warrior here."

"I know. Thank you, doctor."

"Right," La Loca says as soon as the doctor is gone. "Let's get to work. You can take notes, Tomas, and make suggestions. I'll work out a routine around the chorus. You, Angelita, keep going on the piano."

Time passes slowly. Tomas's wounds are healing well, a process that cannot be rushed. La Loca sets up a small space at the bottom of the garden obscured by trees. There she practices her moves for the dance section of the chorus. I work every day, but I'm not happy with it. Something is missing, a sound, a force, a passion that will express the anger and sorrow of the incarcerated women. I wander about the house, touching things, gazing out at the trees, thinking.

*

The next day, I return to my father's house. It is early morning. I let myself in with my key and tiptoe to the salon. He sits gazing out of the window, his back to me. My hands are slippery with sweat, the key slides from my grasp and clatters to the floor. He turns.

"Angelita, darling! I was not expecting you! How long have you been here? How did you get to Madrid?"

"I was here before," I say shortly.

"Before? What do you mean, before? When?"

"Three months ago. When I first got to Madrid. You were in your study, working. I went to the salon to wait for you."

His face creases in puzzlement. "But… but I didn't see you. Why did you not wait, not say something—"

"I saw the papers on your table," I interrupt. "I read them."

My father's face is a mixture of puzzlement and fear. "You have no right to—"

"I have every right! You talk about rights, Papa? What about all those women? What about their rights? They have none! You made sure of that, didn't you?"

He comes towards me. "Angelita, you don't understand—"

"Oh, I understand only too well! You tortured, raped, murdered, took away all humanity and dignity, you killed the innocent—"

I turn away in disgust. I feel my face grow hot, my voice shakes, my stomach a clenched fist. I feel sick. "Did you enjoy it? Did it make you feel alive, powerful? Stop! Don't come near me! I read the papers. I know what you did."

"You don't know! You cannot know what I did, and you can never know why."

"Stop speaking in riddles. Just be honest with me, for once! You signed those papers, didn't you?" He turns away without answering. "All these years you've been lying to me. But I'm older now, Papa, old enough to know the difference between your fictions and reality. I know now why my mother left you—"

"Don't talk about your mother as if—"

"And why she can't bear to talk about you, wants to shove you into the background. You never gave her a choice. You say you love her. love me. What does that mean? What is love to you? You have no *idea* what love is, deep, imperfect, real love. Stay back! You are as close now as you will ever be to me. I know the truth now, why everyone went silent if I mentioned your name. I will never forgive you for what you did to my mother, to all those women, to me—the lies, the fake affection—"

"It is not fake affection!" his voice trembled, face suffused, contorted. "I love you. You are my child—"

"You thought you could own me, set me against my mother and Orlando," I choke back tears, grab my bag and make for the door. "All you did was impregnate my mother! Don't try to deny what's in those documents. I know everything now."

"I don't deny what is in the documents. But there is a reason."

"That's what I thought." I open the door into the street. "Goodbye, Papa."

"This will never be over," he calls after me, voice trembling, "Not for you, not until you have learned the truth… if you ever do."

I stumble into the street. The air feels hot, stifling. I wipe away the sweat that forms like tears on my forehead and walk blindly, without direction, oblivious to the noise of traffic, the murmurs of the life I have left behind, crushed by a sense of emptiness and loss.

I make my way back to Joaquin's house, the image of the vulture in the garden hovering over me. I shudder. The heaviness in my father's house sits in my chest like a stone. I lean on a wall and force myself to breathe. I am aware of people staring and force myself to move forward, away from that street, away from that house, away from the man I have loved all my life. And I know the empty space inside me can never be filled.

*

The work for our first performance is well underway. La Loca practices daily behind the trees in the garden. Every few days, we come together to rehearse the final routine. We are almost ready. With the help of trusted colleagues, Joaquin has secured a safe place and a carefully selected audience. The performance will take place in a large, abandoned space, an ancient cemetery on the outskirts of the city. We get together for the final planning.

"What happens if something goes wrong?" La Loca asks. "What if the Falangists find out, get tipped off or something? Then what?"

"There's an out," Joaquin assures us. "A quick exit leading to the fields and lane behind. Two vehicles will be waiting. Also, we'll have men posted at points around the cemetery to signal any approach."

"We have to be sure we can protect Lidia Falcon," I say.

"She's well known, recognizable. We must sure she's not seen before the performance."

"Lidia Falcon the poet?" Tomas is impressed. "How did you meet her? She's a wonderful poet, also a lawyer—"

"Yes, and involved in politics too. The government are on the lookout for her. We have to be careful," I say. "If she's caught, it's all over. She won't stand a chance."

"There's always a chance," La Loca puts in. "Always. That's why we're here, isn't it?"

"Right. Let's go over the script," Joaquin suggests.

"What about lighting?" Tomas asks.

"Lanterns, lots of lanterns, all over the area, but screened from the valley and the road by sheets of bamboo. Only those who've been told and invited will see them. We'll need a lot of them," I say. "So yes, Tomas, can you be responsible for that?"

"Let's have a look at the plan, the script," Joaquin says again. His voice is tense. I glance at him curiously.

I spread a large sheet of paper over the table. "Here's the gate where people will come in. There's where you'll stand, La Loca, behind those pillars before you start to dance. Myself and the chorus of women, and then Lidia Falcon, will enter from these points. The guitarists will sit over there, to either side of the space so they can be heard. The women will interweave among the watchers. I'll be among them."

"Looks good. Not too much noise. too much light. Just enough." Joaquin nods.

"So, a woman emerges slowly from the darkness—that's you, La Loca—dressed in a flowing red dress. Your naked body can be seen in outline underneath. You move silently at first among the gravestones. You pause by one of the lanterns. That's when you begin your dance. There's flamenco guitar in the background—you'll need to practice with them. Then you stop and look directly at the watchers, extend your arms as though in supplication. Your hands look like two white doves caressing the darkness. One more short dance. Then you move slowly backwards and disappear.

"Then what?" everyone says at once.

"Then this. The script for the voices. I've called it *The Cemetery of Forgotten Women*. Someone will announce that. Look it over," I say as I spread the script on the table.

THE CEMETERY OF FORGOTTEN WOMEN

First Woman: There's a new one coming in. Have to pay special attention to her.

Second Woman: Have to be careful not to damage her.

First Woman: You know what that means, of course.

Second Woman: Gently, to make sure she's a virgin.

First Woman: Shouldn't be too difficult. Where's this one from?

Second Woman: They found her at home in Valladolid while they were searching for her brother. I'm surprised she got off lightly. Beautiful little thing.

First Woman: She's for the generals. the guards had orders not to touch her.

Otherwise, they'd have raped her.

Second Woman: The generals don't like damaged goods.

First Woman: No, they like fresh meat.

Second Woman: Pigs!

First Woman: Ssshhh! Careful!

There's a shout, a scream, sounds of boots.
Two soldiers enter carefully bearing girl in red dress.

First Soldier: You know what to do.

Second Soldier: She's beautiful.

Second Woman: Hands off this one! Special order for one of the generals.

First Woman: Otherwise, you'd have worn her out by now!

Second Woman: Filthy bastards!

Second Soldier: One of the perks of the job, old woman! Nothing like a bit of fresh pussy on a hot day to get the juices flowing, and plenty of it around, free for the taking.

First Soldier: Especially since the boss has made the whorehouses off limits.

Second Soldier: *(to First Woman)* How about a quickie, old girl?

First Woman: You disgust me!

Second Soldier: Well, beggars can't be choosers!

First Soldier: Come on, we have to get going, anyway. a new batch coming in soon.

Second Soldier: *(to First Woman)* I'll see to you later, old crone!

Soldiers exit stage right.

Women lay girl on gravestone, stand back to one side.
Girl in red sits up slowly, looks around.

Girl in Red: They said I was too pretty to kill or send away, and to get me ready for the generals. It's a big building right in the city centre. They call it the Cemetery of Forgotten Women. Nobody knows what happens to all of them. I'm scared, don't want to go there!

First Woman: We'll take care of you, dear.

Second Woman: Make sure you come to no harm.

Girl in Red: Are they going to hurt me?

First Woman: *(strokes Girl's cheek, kisses her).* You're safe for
now.

Second Woman: We have our orders, you see. We'll be gentle.

They lay the girl down on the gravestone, shield her with
voluminous garments, begin a slow movement around her.
Lantern extinguished.
Enter stage right,
General dressed in pale grey:

General: Where is she? I was told she'd be ready!

Voices are heard all around the space. There is an
overlapping, echo effect.

Voice 1: Here!

Voice 2: Here!

Voice 3: Here!

Voice 4: Here!

General: Where? Where? Who are you?!

Voice 1: We are the voices of the women!

Voice 2: All the women you have raped!

Voice 3: All the women you have tortured!

During the following chorus, shadows and
reflections flit wraithlike around the graveyard.

Chorus (sung):
We are all the women you have hidden
Hidden in the Cemetery

The Cemetery of Forgotten Women.
But we have not forgotten,
We are the witnesses.
We know
That you have poisoned our land
Killed our children in the womb
Tortured our brothers
Bestowed freedom on killers,
On those who feed
On the suffering of others,
On the anguish
Of their own people.
We are the witnesses!
WE KNOW
That you are drawn to darkness,
That all light blinds you,
That the tree of life is there
For you to maim and slash.
With your mouths to the bark
You suck away the holy life.
BUT WE KNOW
You will choke on the nectar you have culled
From the blood of innocents.
A thousand serpents
Will plague your nightmares
In a labyrinth of torture.
WE ARE THE WITNESSES!
Cry mercy to the ears of justice
Deafened by your blows!

Enter Soldier, stage right.

Soldier: Come with me, Your Honour.

General: LEAVE ME!

Soldier: But, Your Honour, it is not safe. Come with me.

Voice 1: Leave him!

Voice 2: He belongs here!

Voice 3: He and his kind belong here!

Voice 4: They are the living dead!

Girl in Red rises, walks to General. Soldier, backs away, and exits stage right. Flamenco guitar.
Girl in Red encircles General, ensnares him in filmy red dress.
Enter stage left, First Woman, moves to head of tombstone. Enter stage right, Second Woman, stands at foot of tombstone.

First Woman: It's risky. If they find out, you know what they—

Second Woman: They will kill us, taking their time.

First Woman: A bit at a time until we're half dead.

Second Woman: I'm already half dead. You take the feet,

First Woman: And you the arms, the head.

They lay General on tombstone, wrapped in red.
Girl in Red stands naked except for red mask, watching Women lower General into the tomb.
Girl in Red begins wild dance of joy and liberation
Dances on the tombs and among the watchers.
Finally, stage centre, faces audience, arms raised in gesture of triumph, vanishes into shadows, throwing red mask onto stage centre. The two

*women have drifted offstage. All that remains is
the red mask, enclosed in a circle of bright light.
There is a short stroke of flamenco guitar.
Voices begin in chorus, reverberating in audience.*

Chorus YOU ARE THE WITNESSES! You the people!
First Voice: The power is here, with you!
Second Voice: You have the power!
Third Voice: Power to transform the trails of terror!
Fourth Voice: To end the pathways of evil!
Chorus: Our land is a broken warrior
A warrior who can move
And be reborn.

Single guitar stroke.
BLACKOUT

All lanterns extinguished.

*

We stand looking at each other. La Loca weeps, shrugs when someone puts a hand on her arm, dries the tears and stands erect and silent, one arm raised high, fist clenched. She looks like a statue I have seen once in Madrid, before it was demolished, a warrior woman of the revolution.

"Where do we go from here?" says Tomas quietly.

"To the cemetery," I reply. "It's time to set up there, get used to the space." The others nod assent.

eight

EVERYTHING IS IN PLACE. LANTERNS ARE LIT, AND everyone is ready back in the darkness. The watchers arrive and settle among the tombs. At the gate stands Tomas, scrutinizing the people as they come in, receiving the cards they hand him, which he also scrutinizes carefully.

My heart pounds. I will have to go back there soon to join the singers. I smooth my fingers over the gold medallion Tomas had given me. *Libertad.*

As La Loca finishes her impassioned flamenco dance and disappears, my gaze is drawn back over the wall to the fields, a tiny flash of light, quickly gone, like moonlight on a silver buckle or a swiftly vanishing star. I look about for Joaquin but cannot find him in the darkness. I turn back to the improvised "stage" at the back of the cemetery, a long flat space between two tombs. The Girl in Red has melted into the darkness her white hands like fluttering doves in the dimness, her red mask alone now in a pool of red light.

"Blood!" someone whispers. "Blood!"

Lidia appears, picks up the mask and stands in silence, holding the mask in front of her. There is a collective gasp, a stirring among the watchers.

"It's Falcon!" someone whispers. "Lidia Falcon, the poet!"

Lidia looks small and vulnerable in the lantern light between the towering tombs, but her voice rings out in the night.

"Many of you know me as a lawyer, novelist, dramatist and poet. I am an activist working for the rights of women in Spain and in the world. I have been imprisoned for my views. What you may not know is that my entire family have been executed or exiled for their opposition to this fascist regime. None of these injustices will stop me in my fight for freedom, for the rights of women, and founding the Feminist Party. I will work tirelessly to legalize abortion and divorce, the right to vote, to own property, to be educated. Read my journal. *Vindicacion Feminista*. Join me!"

She holds up the mask with both hands, then throws it to the floor.

"Join us! You have power. You have influence. Together we can unmask this corrupt regime!"

I think she has finished, but she raises a clenched fist.

"Poder y libertad!" she cries and, turning abruptly, disappears into the darkness.

I feel a tug on my sleeve. "We have to get out of here!" La Loca cries as she runs. "Before they surround us! Move!"

I look about in alarm. Most of the watchers have left through the gates. Across the fields, a steady movement is discernible in the dim light of early stars. How did they know? I move towards the gates and the truck waiting in the lane, trip and fall, get up and scramble towards the gates. Four strong hands grab my arms and slam me into the wall. Darkness.

I awake in freezing blackness to a murmur of distant voices, the scurry of some creature over the floor. Across a high window, a dusky shadow flits. The door-lock rattles. I try to lift myself up, but my hands are tied behind me.

"Don't try to sit up," a familiar voice says. "Let me help you. I'll undo the ropes."

He sits beside me on the hard bed. I cannot not see him in the dark, but I know the voice, the touch, the familiar musky mixture of sweat and soap and need. I sit up, massage my wrists and force myself to breathe deeply. I pull away from the hand on my back. Thoughts tumble through my head, and I will myself to control the rising panic. His voice. What in God's name has happened? And why?

"Why?" The word is out, no time to think. Too much thinking, not enough answers, confusion and darkness, the unknown and unexplained, are beginning to overwhelm me. I freeze and sit in silence.

"Someone told them. That's why. I managed to get the others away just as we planned. But you... we couldn't see you, thought you must have gone ahead with Lidia Falcon. We left, and they found you." He moves to put his arm around me. I shrink.

"The others..."

"In the safe house."

A fumbling at the door.

"Leave us," Joaquin instructs the guards.

"Of course, sir." Door clangs shut, and footsteps recede.

"Where am I?"

"It's the Cemetery of Forgotten Women, the place I told you about. I know it well and know a way out. I will take you there, but we have to wait until everything is quiet. This is not a prison. It's the holding area, before they take them up to the rooms where they are groomed for the generals.

"I'm not going *there!*"

"No, you are not. I'll see to that. I'll have you out of here by nightfall. But now I have to leave."

The sun breathes on the high window. I pull myself up to look out. Nothing. Just a small empty yard. I move to the door and try the handle. The door opens into the dark silence of the hall. A pungent miasma slides over me, an odour of despair. I raise my hand to brush it away and drop it, knowing the despair is my own. I feel my way down the hall, peering into each cell. All empty. I think of all the women everywhere, their fear, their distress, and my heart aches for them. I sing softly.

Nunca olvidara/never forget/the music that echoes in the souls/of the unheard/nunca olvidara/inside the hollow place of your fear/flourishes the midnight flower/of your courage/and as it opens/you are free.

A movement ahead in one of the cells. I feel my way along the walls and peer in. A young woman sits alone in a slice of sunshine, reading. I tap on the door. She looks up quickly, surprised, frightened, then beckons me in. We sit side by side, in silence at first.

"Who are you?" I ask. "And why are all the cells empty and the doors unlocked?"

"Isabella Torres. They're waiting for a new consignment of girls. The doors are unlocked because there's no way out of here, nowhere to go. What's your name?"

"Angelita de Caballe. I don't believe there's no way out. There is always a way out."

"Not unless you have the plans, and few do. De Caballe, you say? You are Bruno de Caballe's daughter? You must be so proud of him. He saved so many of us before we were brought here to the cemetery. But they found out and took him in. I heard they tortured him horribly before he confessed."

"Confessed?"

The young woman speaks breathlessly without stopping as if to expel a poisonous taste. "They used him as cover for General Montelban. Sadistic bastard that one, took real pleasure watching the rapes and mutilations. I heard he was particularly attracted to the dead ones. But it was Bruno who paid the price. Franco had to do something. Other governments were watching, opponents and allies alike. He demanded a confession. Bruno gave in after they threatened to kill his daughter. He wrote and signed the confession. They say he's retired now. That's an understatement. I saw him just before they caught me after a Lidia Falcon rally. He couldn't move without a crutch. Then the bastards came up with this idea, the Cemetery of Forgotten Women. Here they're pampered and made ready for the generals. Virgins get special treatment. But they never leave." She gasps, stops abruptly, stares at my eyes. "Oh God, I'm so sorry… your father… I shouldn't have… I needed to talk… I wasn't thinking… I am so sorry… it's so lonely here…"

I can't speak. I get up and leave.

The sun shifts, the cell grows cold. Still Joaquin has not returned. I stare at the closing eye of fading light on the ceiling, see my father's face there. A sob chokes my throat. I swallow. The creeping cold pierces my skin yet my forehead is wet and hot, moisture drips into my eyes.

Oh, Papa, how... how could I not have known, not have guessed! All my life I've known your warmth, your love, your steadfast belief in me. I know you! You confessed to save me. Where are you now, Papa, in your suffering, your terrible loss? Are you alone? How can you forgive me? But I know of course you will, I know you will, even in your pain and loneliness you will forgive... and... I... I cannot even... cannot even come to you now.

I lie face down on the hard mattress. My limbs are heavy, rigid. All feeling gone. A paralysis of grief. Is this what death is, just a closing down, sleeping on...

The door opens. A voice. A familiar voice. I've heard it before somewhere... somewhere... somewhere... I burrow my face into the mattress, deep into the stink of it.

"You'll need to get up, darlin.'"

I lie still.

"It's Seamus, the one who saw you in the woods when you were doin' your wee experiment with boyhood."

I twist my head slowly. It feels heavy, my neck tight, like turning a steel screw. My throat feels full of gravel. I choke the words out. "Joaquin is..."

"I've seen him, got the plans. That's why I'm here. Get up."

"Seamus? O'Brien?"

"Aye, the same."

My neck creaks towards him "But... how did you get in?"

"Och, just the famous Irish charm and a stubborn refusal to listen to idiots. There's not much time. Up with you. *Rapido. Vamanos.*"

I struggle robot-like to move my limbs. Seamus takes me under his arms and lifts me up. There's a curious gentleness about him, a delicacy that doesn't go with his rough exterior. He places his coat around me, takes my hand and leads me through the door into the darkness. Our journey is long and winding, a journey I could not have made on my own, frozen, legs like wooden planks, blank-minded after the red-haired girl's revelation. The passages smell of damp earth and rot. A heavy silence closes in around us. We must be underground. Something splashes into our path just ahead. We stop and walk gingerly around it.

"Nothin' to worry about," Seamus reassures me. "Just a clump of earth from above. It's not cavin' in."

I'm not worried. Nothing worries me now. I am walking with machine-like stolidity, his arm carefully around me, guiding me.

"Yer in shock, lass, just hold on."

I feel as though time stands still. My mind has given over to just moving forward. It seems a very long way. But at last, a tiny light appears in the distance. As we approach, I see movement there and my body tenses. Seamus tells me someone he knows waits there.

"I have to get back…"

"You can't go back, not to Joaquin's. Too risky. La Loca and Tomas are waiting for you at the safe house. Trust me."

Trust is all I have left.

nine

THE TUNNEL WIDENS, THE PINPOINT OF LIGHT expands and I see a familiar shape silhouetted against the daylight. My heart pounds, relief overwhelms me. I clutch at Seamus's arm, and he steadies me. My eyes brim with tears at the sound of the wolf. I run towards the exit, stumble and fall.

"Steady on, lass, easy now," says Seamus from behind me. I ignore him, fling myself into Tomas's arms. He winces, still raw from his wounds. Behind him, La Loca is beginning a spontaneous flamenco dance of jubilation, then stops and flings her arms around me in a tight embrace.

"You took your time," she says. "Damn fool, we thought we'd lost you."

"We have to move fast," Seamus warns, "before it's too light and the Guardia patrol the area." We fall in behind him like soldiers as he leads the way out of what appears to be a maze of trees and trenches, clearly the remains of a battle site. There is a large lake ahead; Seamus leads us carefully around it, warning us to watch out for mud. "It'll suck y'in, and that'll be the end of ye."

After what feels like a long time, he stops. "Sshh, quiet. Down." As he says this, he unslings his rifle, falls on his stomach. We lie flat. I seem to spend a lot of time burrowing into sand and earth and giggle. Seamus frowns and raises his finger to his lips. There are voices up ahead. After a few minutes, two Guardia march perilously close, rifles slung over their shoulders. Seamus shifts slightly, ready to take aim. No need. Within minutes they are shapes in the distance heading towards the city. There's a collective sigh of relief, followed by a warning from Seamus not to get up yet. There may be others. We freeze, breathe deeply and look at each other in silence.

After a few minutes, La Loca gets up and dances.

"Get down!" Seamus hisses, "You could be seen from a distance, movin' like that!"

We wait half an hour until we are sure there is nobody coming, and slowly get to our feet. Seamus and La Loca also rises.

"Let's get going," Seamus says. La Loca links her arm in his, and they move forward together. Tomas and I follow behind, look at each other, nod at the two ahead and smile. It's two hours before we reach the safe house. It's in a narrow back street in a suburb not far from the city centre. Seamus leads us up a dark staircase to the second floor. There are sounds behind doors on the first floor as we pass, hushed voices or whispers. I wonder who it is behind those doors, whether they're Resistance like ourselves. We enter a wide light-filled room with large windows overlooking the street. Seamus shows us the other rooms in the apartment, three of them, each containing two single beds. There's a kitchen and a small bathroom. La Loca and me dump our rucksacks in the first room nearest the bathroom. Tomas takes another room, and Seamus has the third room to himself.

Seamus is cooking bean and potato stew in the kitchen.

I sit down and immediately ask him about the people on the first floor.

"Republicans. Part of the International Brigade. They will probably join our group."

"We should consult with the others in our group before doing that."

"Dinner first. Then, we talk."

We sit all together around the round table, eating and talking.

"There's someone I want you to meet," Seamus tells us. "A singer, *Gitano* like you, La Loca. He sings flamenco and protest songs of his own. I'm taking you tonight to where you can hear him."

I'm intrigued; another singer performing protest songs. A *Gitano* as well! "But how does he get away with it?" I ask. "*Gitanos* are hounded by the government, imprisoned or executed. Are you saying he sings openly, in public?"

"This one's different," Seamus says. "He's famous all over Europe and overseas. Franco has accepted him as a showcase of Spanish culture to Europeans, and to other countries as well. This singer has performed in New York City, London, Milan and Paris. He's in demand. Franco overlooks his ethnicity because of his fame and the attention it brings to Madrid."

"Where's he from? What's his name?" Tomas enquires.

"A small place in Andalucia—La Isla—his name is Camaron. You'll meet him tonight. Don't worry. I've arranged it. It's safe. You'll all be part of his *cuadro*, his group, in theory anyway."

We enter a club in a narrow side street of Madrid's city centre. Seamus talks briefly to a man at the door. The man consults a paper, nods, and lets us in. The large round room is dark except for candles set on shadowy round tables, most of them occupied. Seamus guides us to a table close to the side of a small stage set with two chairs, a small table between them. There is no sign of Camaron. We wait. A waiter brings a bottle of Rioja and four glasses. People around us are drinking and talking in low voices.

After half an hour a guitarist appears. The audience falls silent. The guitarist strikes a chord. A young, fair-haired man appears from behind a curtain and sits. He listens intently to the guitarist for a few minutes and sings, rapping his knuckles on the table between them to the rhythm of the song. His eyes are closed, face contorted as if at some painful memory. I am transfixed. Sounds emerge from his throat that are full of pain, reproach, passion, and anger. He sings from a place inside him, his soul, his heart, some place he can only reach through music. On his face, a look of agony, actual physical pain. Two dancers appear, skirts swirling, feet moving, tapping, stamping in time to the music, arms and hands raised in expressive undulating movements

After a few minutes, he stops singing and accompanies the dancers with *las palmas*, clapping rhythmically to their movements. The dancers leave. He sings another song. Eyes closed, he claps softly to the words, a slow, throaty tale of loss and pain. I glance over at La Loca. Without looking at me, she rises in silence and moves onto the stage, eyes fixed on the singer. She dances. Camaron's eyes open wide as he watches, her movements coordinated to the passion of his words, her eyes black and deep as she turns to look far out into the audience at a vision only she can see. Camaron's words follow her, seem to enter her body as she dances. The song peaks to a howl, a cry of rage, then subsides abruptly. La Loca follows the words and rhythm, stops abruptly with a flourish of arms and hands, skirt swirling, and leaves the stage.

Camaron and the guitarist bow and leave the stage. The waiter brings more wine. "Is it over?" I ask breathlessly.

"Later. More now," Tomas says.

A man emerges from behind the stage and approaches La Loca. "Camaron would like to meet you, senorita. Please, follow me."

La Loca is gone for some time. I look at Seamus, then at Tomas, wondering if we should go to find her. Seamus shakes his head, Tomas nods. We wait.

At last, La Loca reappears and sits. "He wants me to be his dancer," she says, her eyes full of light. She looks entranced. "He wants to practice after the show."

"Oh practice, is it?" Seamus quips. "Sure, ye'll get plenty o' that."

We glance at each other. We know of Seamus's attraction to La Loca, protective and somehow always near her, and now, the green-eyed monster? Jealous of Camaron?

"That's a great honour," I tell La Loca, "and you'll learn a lot, things we can use later on."

Seamus turns away. "Och to be sure, she'll learn a lot!"

La Loca places her hand on his arm. "You idiot," she whispers, "don't you know you're the one for me? And anyway, he's married with four kids."

Tomas and me glance at each other, but say nothing.

"And ye think that bans him from other women!" Seamus retorts.

"Oh, get a hold of yourself!" La Loca fires at his back. "You know nothing about *Gitano* culture!"

"He's a man!" Seamus snaps. "I'm thinking like a man! I know how men think!"

"And you think I don't? After what I've been through in Malaga?"

Seamus turns suddenly, pulls La Loca into the darkened side of the stage and kisses her on the lips. She doesn't resist. "I know, darlin', what you've been through. Are ye not knowin' yet that I love ye? And I don't want harm to come to ye."

"I know Seamus. I love you too. But I'm not a prisoner to love."

"What does that mean?"

"Work it out." She kisses him on the lips, turns and rejoins us.

"Are ye meetin' him later then?"

"Of course."

"I'll see y'all back at the house, then." Seamus turns and walks out of the club.

We sit down, stunned by unfolding events. We look at La Loca. She shakes her head and shrugs. I am seeing a side of her that is new to me: independence, confidence that has been lacking before. Has this all come from her encounter with Camaron, or was it obliterated in Malaga and re-emerging now in a revelation of her true character? Whatever it is, there is a change in her, and it is connected to her passion for dance. I understand that. She has a rare gift, an ability to move people through music and her body's grace. I move to sit beside her.

"Whatever you decide, my friend, I'm there for you," I tell her.

"I know," she says quietly, places her arms around my shoulders and kisses me on the cheek.

The lights dim. The guitarist returns to the stage. Two dancers enter, and he watches them closely, improvising to their movements. This is their moment to shine, and he illumines their talent with his own sensitivity and musical genius.

After a time, the dancers exit and the guitarist plays alone. He stops suddenly.

Camaron enters. He sings a *bulerias,* haunting and slow at first, building to a shout, a cry, his arm raised, fist clenched. It is a song of protest. There is an explosion of applause from the audience. I notice three Guardia standing at the back. They are enthusiastic. I wonder if they would applaud if Franco had not sanctioned the singer. It doesn't matter. This is inspirational, a triumph, and the people are moved.

I turn to La Loca. "You'd be insane not to work with this man." Staring at the stage as if hypnotized, she nods imperceptibly.

The performance ends to wild applause. Camaron has great dignity. He bows and slowly exits the stage.

We move towards the exit. The Guardia stand aside. Outside, we realize La Loca is not with us. She has stayed behind to be with Camaron, as we knew she would. We make our way back to the safe house, carefully avoiding the Guardia patrolling in pairs in the main thoroughfares and side streets. We arrive without incident. We haven't eaten all day and are starving, raiding the refrigerator for cheese and milk and fruit. There's wine on a side table. Satiated, make our way up to the bedrooms.

I pause at my door and turn to smile at Tomas. "How are your burns?" I say softly. "You could lie quietly beside me. I won't hurt you."

We take off our clothes and lie under the cool sheet of my bed. We are both exhausted by the emotion of the evening and fall asleep, touching. Some time during the night, I awaken, turn to Tomas, snuggle into his chest and place a hand on his stomach.

He stirs, puts his arm around me, and looks into my eyes in the dim light of the street lamp. "I love you, Angelita," he whispers.

I slide closer, careful not to touch his wounds. I feel like a flame is melting us together, closer than we have ever been. We lie together and look into each other's eyes. He touches my face, strokes my hair. I am gentle with him, for I know he still has much pain. I long to feel him inside me, making love to me with the passion and need we both feel. I move between his legs and kiss him softly. He strokes my head as my lips enclose him, eyes closed as he moves to my rhythm, becomes rigid and cries out as he reaches orgasm. My throat fills with a soft sweet taste of honey. I swallow and kiss him gently, kiss him gently and endlessly until again he moves rigidly against me. Into the night I kiss him, again and again until we are both exhausted. We sleep.

ten

L A LOCA APPEARS MID-MORNING. SHE LOOKS invigorated. We look at her questioningly.

"What?" she laughs. "Nothing happened. Not what you think, anyway. You should know, Tomas, the *Gitano* family code."

I turn to Tomas.

He nods. "Loyalty to family. Fidelity."

"But—"

"I know, but he's a man. He's away from home. Nobody would know. Except him. He would know."

"It's against his code, his beliefs," La Loca said. "Sex with women other than his wife is taboo, disrespected by his clan. I'm *Gitana*, remember."

"What did you do all night?"

"Worked. Danced. Talked about plans."

"Plans?"

"He wants me to perform with him, starting with New York."

"But, La Loca, what about us? What about *our* plans? What will we do without you? All the performances, everything we've worked for."

"I haven't decided yet. I'm just telling you what we did. But there's something else. Camaron's been asked to sing for Franco. He wants me to dance."

"Camaron has accepted? Where? Is it safe? Would you be… protected? And why would you dance for the tyrant anyway! It's against all you believe in… and what if…"

"What if I'm caught? I won't be. I'd be with Camaron's group. He would shield me. And anyway, I haven't decided yet. But think of this: I could make some important contacts."

"Well, we need to know if you're going to do it. We have another performance coming up, Lidia Falcon will be involved again, and Joaquin is organizing it. If you can't be there…"

"I can. I will. I'm free to make my own decisions. And our group is my priority. I just need to know where and when."

"Joaquin is coming here later, and Lidia. I'll know more then." I turn away to hide the unease I feel. I'm used to being in control, to making the important decisions. I'm not used to insecurity. Tomas puts his hand on my arm.

"Wait. Be patient. There's time. No decisions are made yet." I try to smile at him, but it feels like a mask stretched across my face.

"I'm going out," La Loca says, "to meet a friend. See you later." The door slams.

Later we talk to Seamus. "She loves you, you idiot. Nothing happened. He wants to work with her, that's all. He's been asked to sing for Franco. He wants her to dance"

"What? No! That's out of the question!"

"Seamus, I have to tell you, my friend, it is not your decision."

"But if she's caught, identified…"

"She hasn't decided yet. He wants her to go to New York with the group, but I don't think she wants to."

"You don't think! But what does she think? What about our own work?"

"Seamus, you must be patient. We all must. This is not our decision to make. La Loca is still a free woman. She can make her own decisions."

Seamus nods abruptly, turns away, shoulders hunched. "I'm worried for her safety, d'you see? She'd be going into a den of lions, they could tear her to pieces, the bastards." His hands are shaking.

"If she's part of Camaron's *cuadro,* she'll be safe. Nobody will know who she really is."

"We can't be sure of that! What if someone recognizes her? What if someone has seen her at rallies? What if…"

"Stop, Seamus! All this speculation is getting us nowhere. The decision is not yet made. We have to wait and see."

"Where is she? I'm off to speak with her!" Seamus shouts and leaves. We all know how he feels. The thought of La Loca being at risk puts us all at risk. But she is stubborn, fiercely independent. There's nothing we can do but wait.

"Seamus is a hot-head," Tomas comments, "but if he keeps this up, he'll just drive her to it, you know how stubborn she can be."

"Oh yes, I know, and it is both her weakness and her strength. Look, let's have something to eat, then talk about our plans," I suggest, trying to put some calm into things, some normality, if there is such a thing as normality any more. Events are changing daily. I have a sense of impending doom, but I squash the feeling down and head for the kitchen. The others follow.

We eat in silence, waiting for the door to open below, the familiar slam of La Loca returning.

La Loca flings herself down at the table. "I'm hungry. What's for dinner? I'm not going to New York," she mutters all in one breath.

The relief in the room is palpable. "I'm just going to dance for Camaron," she adds, "when he sings for Franco." There's a frozen silence, a chill of apprehension.

"*Just?*" says Seamus with meaningful irony. "You'll be dancing in front of that bastard, La Loca. That's *just* what you'll be doing!"

"How can you be sure it's safe?" Tomas's face is creased with concern.

We all talk at once. "Is there a way out… do they know your name… how will Camaron protect you… have they seen you dance before… what are you going to do if…"

"Shut up," La Loca says calmly and continues to eat her dinner. "You're giving me indigestion. I've decided. It's a one-off. I'll be part of Camaron's *cuadro*. There'll be other dancers there, I'm just one of them. Mmmm, nice chicken. And yes, there is a way out, and yes, I'll be at our next performance, the one with Lidia. Is there any fruit?"

"You're a cocky lass, I'll say that," Seamus says. "Always up for a challenge, while we're all pissin' ourselves with worry."

"But we're glad you'll be with us at the next performance." I move to sit beside her and put down some strawberries. She breathes in the sweet scent of the berries.

"Been saving these for you."

"When is it, by the way?" Tomas asks.

"When is what?"

"Camaron's stint for Franco."

"Soon. I'll let you know. It's before our next performance anyway."

"I'm coming too," Seamus says suddenly, "as part of the backstage help."

"*No puede ser.* No. You will not."

"But…"

"No. I'd be worrying about what you're doing instead of dancing. The answer is no. It cannot be."

"I'll find a way. I don't need your permission," Seamus snaps and leaves.

*

Our next performance is to be in a huge abandoned warehouse just south of the city. There is a narrow lane running behind it leading to the forest nearby, where help will be waiting if needed. Joaquin has done his magic, inviting important guests. Two aides of Franco's have already committed to join us. But we have to be vigilant since the last time, when someone knew about the performance in the cemetery. The group will meet soon to discuss the performance in detail.

La Loca agrees to dance for us. But first, some time before our event, she is to perform with Camaron at Franco's palace. It is all arranged. There's no dissuading her, no going back.

"I promised," she tells us, "and I never break a promise."

The date is set for two weeks from now.

Seamus speaks privately to me. "I'll be there," he says. "Don't know how exactly, but I'll be there, just in case."

"Just in case what?" I ask. "What is the point of you being there? You'll only make it harder for her."

"I know what I'm doing. I'll mingle backstage. They'll think I'm part of the group, I'll be close by in case anything goes wrong."

I see that he is as stubborn as La Loca, but he's in love with her and won't be talked out of it.

"Be careful," I warn. "If anyone should recognize her, you'll both be jeopardized."

"I know. I'm ready."

"Does she know?"

"Not yet."

"You should tell her."

"Not yet."

I give up. The two of them are a good match: generous, kind, headstrong and stubborn. The time comes, and La Loca leaves the house. Seamus sits unconcernedly at the table until he hears the door bang, then jumps up. He means to follow her all the way and sneak in after her. Camaron and the group will be waiting at the rear door, so he will be assumed part of the group. We sit down together to wait. We'll wait until both return. Tension hovers in the air, a palpable sense of threat, fear of the unknown, awareness of the government's power, and a conviction that this is a bad idea. As the evening wears on, we pretend to be absorbed in a game of cards, but none of us are concentrating. The game is a sham to hide our mounting dread. We know the shows go on long after dark, so we wait. And wait. Beyond the curtain, we see the beginning of the dawn. We give up the pretence and sit staring at each other in silence. A distant bell chimes five. There is a shuffling sound at the door. We leap to our feet and run to the door. Seamus enters. His face is haggard with exhaustion, hair awry. He slumps at the table. We gather round him and wait.

"She's gone," he says tonelessly.

We all speak at once. "Whadya mean, gone? Gone where? What's happened? We thought you were with her…"

He raises his head and shrieks. "GONE!" The sound rises

from his gut, like a tortured animal. He bangs his head on the table.

"Whisky," I say to Tomas. "Fast." We place a large glass of whisky in front of Seamus. He stares, grasps it, and it's gone in one huge gulp. He sobs. He bangs his head on the table again until we hold him back. He continues sobbing, his face ravaged, a wild look of insanity in his eyes. We wait. The distant clock chimes six. He raises his head and stares at us with eyes hollow with grief.

"Someone recognized her. There was nothing I could do, nothing. She just disappeared. The crew made me leave with them. I don't know where she is. She just disappeared, there were Guardia all around. They let us leave, but they took her. They must have taken her. She's gone."

He is raving now, his eyes wild and demented.

I slap his face, hard. "Stop!" I shout. "Stop this! This is not going to help her, pull yourself together and tell us what you remember, and we'll work out what to do!"

He jumps up as if to punch me. Tomas holds his arms, and he flops down with a gesture of surrender.

"Everyone was applauding," he whispers. "Everyone. Especially one of the generals in the front, sitting by Franco. The man got up suddenly and started to dance with her. He could dance well, and he danced her off the stage into the wings. None of the crew saw where they went. They just disappeared into the darkness behind the curtains. Franco went on clapping... and she was... she was gone... The Guardia surrounded the stage until the show finished and Franco left."

My throat is tight and dry. "Where was Camaron?" I ask.

"He was still on stage singing with the guitarist playing.

Two of the other dancers motioned to him that something was wrong and they cut the song short."

"Where did they go?"

"Backstage. Soon after that they left, we all left. I didn't want to. I wanted to find her and bring her with us, but they insisted we all left together so as not to arouse suspicion."

"Suspicion?"

"That we might be involved with her, that we were planning something… Someone recognized her."

"Or you," I say abruptly. He looks up at me in shock.

"What? What do you mean, or me? Nobody knew—"

"It was obvious someone knew, someone who had been at the performance when Lidia Falcon was there, someone who recognized you. And La Loca."

"You're saying… you're saying… because of me… she…," Seamus stammers.

"That same person must have known we were there at the cemetery performing!" Tomas whispers, his eyes black and huge with worry. "Joaquin might know. We have to find him!"

"No," I say flatly. "We must wait. All we can do now is wait. That's the hardest part of all this now. Waiting. Sit down, all of you."

eleven

TIME PASSES SLOWLY WHEN THE HEART IS TROUBLED, helplessness a poison in our veins, rendering us sick and silent. We wait for two days. Still no sign of her. Seamus lies in the back bedroom like a sick child, eating nothing, staring at the ceiling, speaking to no-one. I manage to get a message to Joaquin, but there is no response.

Three days pass. No sign of La Loca. Abruptly, the door opens, and Joaquin enters. We leap to our feet, full of questions, anxious to know what has happened.

Joaquin sits down, draws a deep breath, and stares at us. We wait.

"She's been taken."

We all talk at once. "Taken! Taken where? By whom? What's going on? When?"

"The Cemetery," he says abruptly and puts his head in his hands. "They've taken her to the Cemetery of Forgotten Women. Someone recognized her and reported her to Franco's generals. They arrested her." He's mumbling, almost incoherently. I feel he is traumatized by events and his powerlessness to stop them. I move to sit by him, comfort him. Seamus catches my eye, shakes his head quickly. I draw back.

Seamus sits opposite him.

"Who?" His voice is quiet, but in his calm there is threat and tension. He has more to say. "*Who* recognized her? Who told them? You were the only one there that could have known."

Joaquin raises his head, stares at Seamus, his face haggard with fatigue. "No. There was another." He pauses. "You. You Seamus. You told them. When you interacted with her on the side of the stage, they recognized you, and through you, her."

Seamus leaps to his feet and smashes his fist into Joaquin's face. He falls backwards, hits his head on the steel hearth and lies still. For a moment, shock freezes us, then Tomas and I move swiftly to cradle him gently to a bed. Tomas runs for warm water. I turn to find that Seamus has left the room, I hear his swift steps on the stairs to the street.

"Damn him!" I curse. I *told* him to stay away, that they might recognize him. "The foolhardy bastard!"

Tomas puts his arm around my shoulder. "*Querida*, now is not the time for recriminations. Now is a time for calm, to work out a plan and to make sure Joaquin is all right. Get that doctor, the one that helped me." I don't move. "*Now*, Angelita!"

I shake my head violently to clear the sense of deadness and head for the door. I know where the doctor lives and run all the way. It is late, dark already, a thin wisp of light along the horizon like a long sharp knife.

The house is silent. Perhaps he is out or retired already. I thump with all my strength on the door. "*It's Angelita!*"

There is a stirring upstairs, and a light goes on. The doctor appears at the door, rubbing his eyes, coat on over his nightclothes, bag already in hand. "You have a way of making yourself known, my sweet," he quips. "Jump in."

I fill him in as he drives. He parks in a side street, takes the stairs in twos and I follow breathlessly. Joaquin's head is still bleeding, his face a yellowish white, but his eyes are open. He cannot move his head. The doctor tells us to leave.

Half an hour passes. My hands are shaking. Tomas holds them tightly in his, and I force myself to breathe deeply. The door opens.

"He'll live," the doctor says, "but he is in great pain. I've given him painkillers and a sedative. But his neck may be fractured. We have to get him to a hospital. Now. Tomas, take this end of the mattress, and I'll take the other. We'll have to slide him down the stairs. Angelita, hold his head very still with this rolled towel. He must move as little as possible as we slide him into the car."

We are told to wait outside surgery. After three hours, the doctor reappears.

"He is recovering, but the surgeon says he will need surgery on his spine. He is delirious, keeps muttering one word over and over: *Silla or Stella.* He's incoherent."

I leap to my feet. "Estella! His little girl! She is alone in their house if the maid has already left! We must go to her, Tomas, immediately!"

"Get in the car," the doctor says.

The house is in darkness except for one low light in the hallway.

I rap on the door, not too loudly so as not to alert neighbours. No response. I try to whisper her name through the door, give my name, and tap gently. There is a sob on the other side of the door, and it flies open. We enter quickly and turn the light off. I sweep the child into my arms and hold her close.

"Papa hasn't come home," she sobs. "It's dark, and I'm all alone and I don't know where he is!"

I take her into the kitchen still holding her close and look around the room. No sign of cooked food. The stove is cold. "Have you eaten, darling?" I ask.

She shakes her head. "Not hungry. I'll eat when Papa comes home."

"He's probably had to work late," I lie, indicating the stove to the doctor. He opens the refrigerator, takes out some eggs, milk and bread and prepares the food.

"He's never late," Estella says. "We always have dinner together." She's calmer now and snuggles into my arms.

"If he's not back by the time we finish this meal, we're going to find out why he's late," the doctor says kindly. "So, eat up."

Estella smiles and picks at the food. "I like cheese with my eggs," she tells him.

"Coming right up," he laughs and takes cheese from the refrigerator. "Here we are! Anything else, Your Majesty?"

Estella giggles and eats enthusiastically.

"Can we play some songs while we wait?" she asks. "I've got a new one. Papa likes to hear my new songs."

"Let's practice it when we've finished dinner," I suggest.

She nods. "All right. May I have some *postre?* I love sweet things. There's cake in the cupboard."

"When you finish the eggs," the doctor says.

We finish the food as I think about how to get Estella calmly out of there and to our safe house. She's sensitive and senses the tension in the room. She looks from me to the doctor enquiringly.

"Estella," I begin carefully, "I don't want you to be alone here, so I'm going to take you home with me until—"

"No, Angelita, no!" she interrupts. "I'll wait here. I know Papa will be home soon."

I exchange glances with the doctor. He moves to sit quietly beside the child, places his arm around her shoulder, and waits.

She looks up at him. "What is it? Has something happened to my papy?" The doctor hesitates. "Tell me!" she insists, shrugging off his arm. "I won't go anywhere until I see Papa!"

The doctor looks at me, I nod. He turns to the child. "I am a doctor, Estella. Your papa was hurt by someone, and I am helping to take care of him."

"But where is he? Can I see him? Is everything all right? Take me to him!"

"I will try to arrange that, Estella, but you see why we cannot leave you here alone. It is better that you stay with us until your papa can be here with you again."

I can see that Estella is distressed, but she is calmer. "I'll come with you if I can see Papa, and I want to see the person who hurt him!" Her voice chokes as she fights back tears. "You have to promise that!"

"I promise you will see him," I tell her. "And I never break a promise. Let's go." We pack up some of her clothes, a photograph, and a violin.

"I won't need all this stuff," she tells me, "because I'll be back soon. Is there a piano at your house?"

"No, there isn't, but we can get one," I tell her, wondering how I'll do that.

twelve

THE CHILD IS IN GOOD HANDS IN THE SAFE HOUSE. Tomas will take care of her while I am gone. I make my way to the prison where La Loca is locked up. I dress carefully in my most attractive dress, hair carefully brushed. I walk to the place and stand outside. I look up at the barred windows and for a moment, my resolve falters. But I know there is only one way. I walk up to the guard at the door and tell him I'm there to visit a prisoner. He turns away.

"Are you sure? You'd better be, because once you're in there, no guarantee you'll get out."

I know that voice! I stare in disbelief. How can it be. It's not possible! Seamus turns back to me and grins.

"All things are possible if you know how and have the guts. Come with me."

"But how? The uniform, the…"

"Shut up, lass. The less said the better. I'll take you to her."

Thankful that he speaks fluent Spanish, I follow. At the cell door stands another guard. Seamus tells him he is to guard the front door and that he will stand guard while Seamus put this new prisoner in. The guard salutes and leaves. I peer through the cell window. There are two narrow beds with thin blankets. La Loca lies on one bed, face to the wall. I tap on the door. No response.

Seamus unlocks the door and shoves me in. "Wait. I'll be back."

La Loca still has not moved. I sit on the other bed and begin a slow flamenco clapping increasing in rhythm and intensity.

La Loca sits bolt upright. "What the... who the hell... Angelita! How did you get in here?" We both jump up, hugging, laughing with joy and sit down together on my bed.

"It was easy. Seamus let me in."

"What? What are you saying!"

"He's crafty. You know that. Somehow, he's managed to get a uniform, looks every bit the real fascist standing at the door. The fact that he speaks fluent Spanish helps a bit, of course." La Loca roars with laughter. "Ssshhh! Don't make too much noise! He says he'll be back."

"'Course he will. He always has a plan, the clever *hijo de puta*! I just hope he lets us in on it soon! Quiet! Someone's at the door!" she cautions.

A key grates in the lock.

"Take these!" Seamus instructs, tossing two blankets at us. "It'll be cold where we're going. And not a sound out of you. Follow me!"

After a few minutes, we know where he's taking us. The dank sour odour of the tunnel assails us as we leave the main corridor. We clutch the blankets close and need no telling to follow closely. We have been here before and know it is risky. But we also know there is an exit. That's what we keep in front of us—freedom.

A clump of earth falls in front of us, and Seamus curses. In the darkness, there is only one light, a small one that Seamus holds downwards behind his back so that we can see. Suddenly there is a groan, and both the light and Seamus disappear. We creep forward cautiously, hands against the earthen wall, and peer into a shallow pit. "Gimme both hands, both of you. I'll count to three. On three, heave!"

My two hands on one arm, La Loca's on the other, on three we heave with all our strength. He falls backwards.

"Knot the two blankets together," he instructs. "That's it. Now throw one end into the pit." He catches the long blankets, ties one end around his waist. "On three, haul as if your lives depended on it!"

We tug and strain, the blankets taut behind us. Suddenly, they loosen. We look behind. Seamus lies panting on the tunnel floor beside us.

"We have to edge round this hole," he tells us. "One at a time, and slowly. Keep ahold of the blankets just in case."

We edge cautiously around the hole. La Loca slips once and regains balance.

"Like this," I tell her, turning to paste myself upright against the wall, sliding slowly past the hole. She follows. Seamus is already on the other side, ready to grab us.

"Christ, that was a close one," he says. "Right, let's go. Slowly. Follow the light."

"Put the light in front of you, and swing it from left to right," I tell him. "Then you can see any holes, and we can follow the light swinging from left to right."

"Clever lass," he laughs and moves ahead, swinging the light. We wrap the blankets around us and follow with caution. He stops suddenly. "Quiet! Listen." Far behind us, there is movement and sounds of voices. "Damn! I hope they fall in the hole! That'll give us time to get out. Let's go."

The saying *there's light at the end of the tunnel* takes on a new significance for us. We are exhausted, freezing despite the blankets, the damp cold of the surrounding earth makes it difficult to even grasp the blankets, and our eyes are strained with the effort to see. No more mistakes are possible. We move forward stolidly, focused a few feet ahead, sliding sometimes in the semi-darkness. Now and then, I reach back to squeeze La Loca's hand, and a fist of frozen flesh nudges back.

"Not long now, lassies," Seamus whispers. "Past the halfway mark."

Halfway mark! I remember the tunnel from last time I made it out. It seemed lighter, warmer, not so far to daylight, not so treacherous. Memory plays tricks when a person is desperate. Of course, it is not warmer or lighter. A little, perhaps. But the stakes were not so high then, nobody pursued us. We were undetected. And had it been springtime, not the grueling bite of winter, the tunnel walls would not be as hard to grip. I pull the blanket around me and focus on the light ahead swinging from left to right. It seems as if we continue like this for hours. But suddenly, there it is: light! Small, dim, distant, but light! I pause briefly and whisper the word back to La Loca. She stops, grunts in reply.

"All right?" I say. Another grunt. We keep moving, shuffling like automatons on the frozen ground, all human feeling abandoned.

This is the way forward, I tell myself, *grunting and shuffling into the future.* I laugh hysterically.

Seamus turns. "Hold on, don't give up now, lass," Seamus says. "Nearly there!"

Grunting and shuffling into the future, I toss back to La Loca. We both laugh, then we can't stop laughing. My belly aches with laughter. I have to force myself forwards.

"Get a hold o' yourselves, lassies!" Seamus shouts. "Hold on a bit longer!"

"We're holding on, laddie!" cries La Loca, choking with laughter. "Holding on!"

"Aye, that we are!" I chime in.

"Women!" we hear Seamus groan, but he never stops moving. We follow stoically, warmed and relieved by laughter and the promise of light at the end of the tunnel.

Suddenly we're there. We tumble out into the morning sunshine, lie flat on our backs, faces to the sun.

"Up!" Seamus orders. "No time to waste. They're behind us." And he walks away in the direction of the safe house.

"Hey, wait for us!" we cry in unison. He keeps moving. We follow, stumbling with fatigue. As we walk, the warmth of the sun touches our bodies, and we breathe in the sweetness of the morning air. The light at the end of the tunnel becomes the road to freedom.

We constantly glance behind us, expecting pursuit. No movement. We're all hoping the same thing. *They've fallen into the hole.* We look at each other and laugh with relief, but keep moving. After a time, Seamus stops, sits down and pulls bread and sausage from a bag, hands some to us. We eat hungrily, washing down the food with the water from Seamus's leather skin bag. Warmed by the sun and food, we lie back to rest.

"Ten minutes," Seamus warns, looking intently behind us. "We're not taking any chances."

"That we're not, laddie," La Loca chuckles. "You've got the monopoly on taking chances with your officer's uniform, the attitude, the whole bundle."

"That whole bundle got us out of there," he responds.

He gets up and crosses to La Loca, pulls her up and kisses her on the mouth. She kisses him back. "Daft bugger," he says, "but I love you."

"Love you too, you fake fascist."

"Right, let's be off."

*

We reach the safe house when the sun is high. We have to be careful and take the side lanes to the house. The welcome is overwhelming. Estella rushes at us, and Tomas holds me close. They have news.

"Papy is recovering!" The words tumble out. "We can go to see him this afternoon!"

We all exchange glances. This will have to be carefully done. We cannot risk more interceptions or more arrests. Confinement is not in our plans. But the girl has to see her father. Someone will have to take her there.

"Let's talk about this later, darling," I say gently. "First, dinner and bed. We'll go see Papy tomorrow."

She nods and throws her arms around me. "I love you, Angelita! You make everything happy, and besides, you can sing!"

I laugh and hug her. "Yes, and we can sing together. But now let's eat."

Later, after Estella is tucked up in bed, we sit around the kitchen table and work out what we must do, how we can do it and still be free.

thirteen

SEAMUS DITCHES HIS UNIFORM. "WELL, IT SERVED ITS purpose," he quips. "Throw the damn thing in the rubbish where it belongs. No, wait, someone might see it. I'll take it out tonight and burn it."

La Loca shrugs. "Pity. Would've been useful for getting into the hospital. Suits you too. I've always had a weakness for a man in uniform."

"I'll need to keep an eye on ye, then. There's lots of them around."

"Not the kind I like." She kisses him and sips her coffee.

"So it's decided then," Tomas says. "I'll take Estella."

I look at him. "Not exactly. It was a suggestion."

"And a good one. The only possible one. All of you have been identified except me. I'll go." He turns as the child comes in. "Nearly ready, *nina*? You'll need a jacket, it's nippy out there today." She hugs him and goes to get her jacket.

I'm worried. "As I recall, it was you that made the suggestion, Tomas. You're aware of what could happen, of course."

"I am."

"And they must not keep the girl."

"No."

"What if they insist on it?"

"We have a plan," he says, without looking at Seamus. We

all know what he means. Seamus always has a plan. We don't ask. Trust is needed here. Estella comes back into the room, flushed with excitement.

"Ready?" Tomas puts out his hand.

"I won't be far behind," Seamus says quietly. Tomas and the child leave. After a few minutes, Seamus follows them down the stairs carrying the discarded uniform. From the window, I can see him place the uniform in a metal container and set fire to it. He stands by the door to make sure it burns, then slowly turns and leaves. Tomas and Estella are some way ahead of him, and he hangs back so that he will not be seen with them as they disappear down the street. As they turn left, he turns right.

I go back to sit at the table with La Loca.

"He always has a plan," I say sardonically.

"Well, the last one worked. Let's hope the next one does, whatever it is."

"All we can do now is wait."

"Yes."

It is very quiet in the house, all the energy seems to have gone out of it, and I miss the friendships, the childish buzz of excitement, the planning and fun. Now a sense of impending disaster pervades the room, but I'm still focused enough to know this is due to my own anxiety. I'm used to pointing the way, being in control. This loss of direction and authority is new to me. I shake my head, roll my shoulders and stretch, to rid myself of the tension taking hold of me.

La Loca moves to the door. "I'm running you a bath, deep and hot, and rubbing warm oil on your shoulders and back. Wait here." I hear water pouring, smell lavender oil, sit back, eyes closed, and sigh.

Relaxed after the warm bath, I lie down under the blankets and fall asleep.

It is already dark when I awaken. A delicious aroma lingers in the air, and I realize I haven't eaten all day. I pull on some clothes and head for the kitchen. La Loca has set the table, and placed a huge pot of stew in the middle.

"Sit. Eat," she commands. I obey eagerly and ladle a generous helping of the *estofado* into my bowl. I chew and swallow with my eyes closed, and a warm feeling of wellbeing washes over me. All is not lost, I think, if we can still have food like this!

When the meal is finished, we sit by the fire looking at each other. We have to do something, we both know that, but we don't know how to go about it.

"If Estella is not back within the next hour, we go to the hospital." La Loca has a grim look of determination about her. "We cannot risk her being taken."

"I'm not sure—"

"I am sure. Both or one of us has to go and get her safely away from there."

"Not you. They know you. You'd be recognized. I will go. I will go in one hour, when it will be getting dark. I'll be less likely to be recognized."

"But, Angelita, think of what you are saying. Getting dark, yes, but inside the hospital it is brightly lit! You will be clearly seen."

"I'll find a way." She knows me well—my courage, my stubbornness—and is silent. We sit unspeaking for an hour as the sun falls out of sight behind the window. A ghostly floating greyness gives way to darkness. I gaze mesmerized through the glass at a tapestry of endless stars. What an exquisite world, this world of endless stars and light, of infinite space and mystery. How did we fall into the darkness engulfing our country, where did the cruelty begin, and why? Was it born in the mind of one hate-filled, cruel, loveless man whose influence over people gave him power, made him feel alive, even loved by some? Or is all this part of some great design, the final throes of an ailing universe, a planet already succumbing to the greed of humankind? *I must write a song about what is happening to us all.* But I cannot bring myself to pick up a pen and write. My mind is elsewhere. I rise, take my coat from a hook by the door and prepare to leave.

*

The hospital is brightly lit. An odour of antiseptic fills my nostrils. I pull a scarf around my head and move to the front desk. "I've come to see Joaquin Montalban."

"You are his wife?"

"No."

"A relative? Only family permitted in at this time."

The nurse turns away, busy with some papers. I glance down the hall and see two Guardia standing outside a door. That must be Joaquin's room. I walk swiftly towards it, unseen by the nurse busy with her files.

At the door, I stop. "Captain Montalban's sister, Selina Montalban. Open the door."

"Identification," says the older Guardia.

"Not necessary." The young Guardia smiles. "The captain's pretty sister would not lie to us. Let her pass." He pushes open the door.

Estella is curled up on the bed beside her father. Tomas jumps to his feet as I enter. I shake my head quickly, he sits.

"Darling," I say to the child, "we must go now. It is late, and your papy needs to rest. We will come again." Estella gazes at her father, who is already asleep, kisses his cheek and slides off the bed.

Outside in the hall, I smile at the younger guard. "My brother is asleep. My fiancé and I are taking my niece home now. She's very tired."

"*Por supesto, senorita. Buenas noches.*" He bows to Tomas.

"*Buenas noches.*"

Some way ahead, a male nurse is pushing a blanket-laden trolley. At the end of the corridor, he turns left. We also turn left, towards the exit. We are almost to the exit when there is a shout some way behind us. "Wait, senorita, you must sign this paper. It is required."

"Run!" I whisper to Tomas. We race for the exit, Estella swinging between us. The exit is barred. A code is needed. The nurse pushing a trolley stops.

"Get on, all of you. Under the blankets and sheets. Now!" I recognize the voice.

Above the mask his blue eyes are bright with urgency. "NOW!" he repeats. We climb on, he covers us and wheels around, back towards the exit as the older Guardia runs past us.

"Have you seen a woman, a man and a child?" he pants.

"No, senor," Seamus replies calmly. "If you'll excuse me, I must get this bundle down to the ambulance area. They are waiting. The Guardia runs on down the hall. Seamus keys in a code, the door swings open, and we're through.

"Now leg it back to the house, and I mean FAST! They're

on to you. I'll follow soon." He unloads the blankets onto a platform and turns back.

We avoid the main avenue and take the back streets to the house, Tomas in front with Estella in his arms. I can barely keep up with them. Sounds of voices far behind us, one rifle shot. No… please no…

"It's a warning shot!" Tomas pants, "A long way off. Keep going."

The door is partly ajar as we reach the house. We push, nearly knocking La Loca over, and tumble in. She locks and bolts the door.

"Upstairs, fast, all lights off. No peering through windows!"

We fling ourselves down in the kitchen, gasping for breath. La Loca places water and juice in front of us, and waits.

"Seamus," I say at last when I can breathe again. Tomas is still cradling Estella, her face buried in his chest.

"What? What do you mean, Seamus? What about him?"

"He got us out. He was in nurse's uniform, and he got us out."

La Loca gets up abruptly and dishes out the supper. "Eat," she commands, "then talk sense."

"I'm telling you, he got us out! He got us out! On his trolley!"

"Where is he now?" Her voice is tight with anxiety.

"At the hospital. They don't know it's him with the nurse's uniform and mask on."

"Well, I told you Seamus always has a plan. What did you expect?" she retorts. But her voice is shaking.

I try to reassure her. "He'll be all right. He'll get out."

We sit in darkness. I take Estella to bed and sit beside her until, exhausted, she falls asleep.

Back in the kitchen, I try to think of a way to release the tension we all feel. "Where can we get a piano?" I ask. They look at me in astonishment.

"A piano?" Tomas is puzzled.

"A *piano!*" La Loca repeats, staring at me in the dim light. "Ahhh. Yes, of course, that's what we need right now, a *piano.* That will solve all our problems!"

"Estella needs one. And we can keep on practicing, working…"

There's a soft tapping downstairs. We creep down and stand listening behind the door. "Open the door, you daft buggers, and let me in!"

We pull the open the door, Seamus glues himself to La Loca. Tomas turns to me, breathing heavily. "What are we going to—"

"No more talking," I say. "Not now. Off to bed, all of us!"

Nobody needs convincing.

fourteen

THE NEXT DAY, WE FIND AN OLD PIANO SITTING ON AN empty lot, strings missing, wood damaged and damp, but we all heaved it up to the flat and made it more or less playable again. Estella helped.

"You were right," La Loca says. "This will keep us all sane while we work out what to do, where to go. And it's good for the girl."

"I have an idea. Something Joaquin told me about some time ago, a place where we would be safe, protected, still able to work. It's not far from Madrid. Many people have had to flee to Germany and France to be free of Franco and to find work, but those who stayed there work the land to provide food for the remaining community."

"This haven you describe, it sounds too good to be true. Where is it? We have to be careful. You know that."

"It's a village."

"A village!" The others look at me in disbelief. "No village anywhere near Madrid is safe!"

"You are wrong. This one is. It's called Marinaleda. It's a communist village. All the people there work, and all are paid the same wage. They live from the food they produce and have cattle."

La Loca turns to the others. "She's finally lost it," she tells them. "It's the stress. What are you saying?" she almost shouts, turning back to face me. "We have to keep our heads. We have to get on with what we can do here, where we are safe."

"Listen to me, La Loca! Yes, we are safe here... for now. But you know very well that we could be discovered at any time. And in Marinaleda there is a community, and protection, and other people to get involved in our work."

"Protection? That close to Madrid? Have you gone mad?" Seamus puts his hand on his lover's arm.

"Let her speak. She knows something, something that could be of use to all of us. Hear her out!" La Loca shrugs, exasperated. Seamus sits down. "We must stay calm. Go on, Angelita, tell us what you know."

"In Marinaleda, there is a history of community. The landowners leave them alone and don't want the land because it isn't arable. We would have to work hard, all of us, for little pay, but enough to live on. All there have equal rights and are paid the same. The people often quote Che Guevara: 'Only those who dream will someday see their dreams converted to reality.' The *alcalde* speaks of *la lucha,* the struggle. Groups of people from the village have gone into food markets, openly taken food to distribute among the poor. Nobody stops them. The police do not stop them. The local gentry gave the people what they saw as fallow, useless land and the people farmed it, changed it. The aristocrats think the people are a bunch of eccentric fools and they don't need the land. So they allowed the village to keep farming."

"But what of our projects, our own work, the writing, the dancing?" La Loca intervenes.

"We can do that there: prepare, work, plan. And we'd be safe from the scrutiny of Madrid."

Tomas looks thoughtful. "Let's decide. We'll take a vote. Raise your hand if you think we should move." He raises his hand. I raise mine, Seamus too, then somewhat hesitantly, La Loca.

"Then it is decided. We move. It's just a question of when." Tomas makes eye contact with me. He knows something is wrong. "What is it?"

I glance at the door to make sure Estella is out of earshot. "What about Joaquin? We know he can't come, not now, perhaps never, we don't know yet. And Estella. What happens to her? Her father is injured and could be crippled, her mother is dead, her only relative left is an aunt, living in England."

There's a long silence while everyone thinks about this. "She can come with us," La Loca says at last.

"Too hard for her. There are children there, but no schools."

"We could teach her."

"I could take her," Seamus says suddenly. "I could take her to England, to her aunt. Can you get the address? No problem with the language. She's bright, and I can teach her basics. Plus, her aunt will be bilingual. The child will be with family. Her father can join her there when... if... he's well enough."

La Loca laughs. Seamus glares at her. "What's funny?"

"You, my love. You always have a plan. This one could work." She plants a kiss on his cheek. "But let's have some details."

"How would you get there?" Tomas says, always the practical one. "Do we have enough money? How would you travel? By train, by ship from Santander? Either way would be dangerous."

"Cargo."

"A cargo ship? How? Where from? Could they be trusted?"

"I have friends in low places," Seamus grins. We laugh in spite of ourselves.

"And while you're off on your cruise, we're working on the land," says La Loca, sardonic as always. "And what about all the other stuff we have to do? How long would you be gone?"

"I have to look into that. Get the address of Joaquin's sister."

"And how do you expect to do that?" I ask. "The address of the aunt? With Joaquin flat on his back, heavily guarded, you can't get near him."

"As I've said, I've friends in… oh, never mind! How do you think I managed to get into the hospital?"

"Now don't tell me you screwed the head nurse!" La Loca laughs.

"No… not quite."

"What do you mean, not quite?"

"All right now, that's enough!" I say. "He got in, and he got us out. *How* he did it is his business. Just be grateful that he did! We're here, aren't we? We're safe. All we have to do now is work out how to get Estella to her aunt in England."

"Yes, boss." La Loca salutes, and everybody laughs.

"Tomas and Seamus, get busy finding out about cargo ships to England. Also be thinking of how you'd get to the ship undetected."

"I've done that already," Seamus interjects.

"Why does that not surprise me?" I say tiredly. "More on that later, then. You and me, La Loca, we're going to Marinaleda to get the lay of the land, to see what's going on there, meet the people, find out about work, accommodations."

"When do we leave?"

"Tomorrow."

"Bit sudden, isn't it?" says Seamus. "I want to spend some time with La Loca before I go. I don't know when I'll be back, thought I'd try to fit in a visit to Ireland, see family, spend a few weeks with them before I come back here."

La Loca puts her arms around him. "I'll miss you, *carino*, so let's make the most of the time we've got. *Buenas noches*, everyone." They link hands and head for the bedroom.

"There won't be much sleeping done tonight, then," Tomas quips.

"On that subject…" I begin.

"You read my mind," Tomas laughs. "Let's get Estella to bed first, then call it an early night." He leaves to see to Estella. I go into the bedroom, peel off all my clothes and lie naked under the sheets. I think of how everything is changing and of all we have to do, my mind going over and over the details. The blankets are comforting and warm, like a soft hand stroking the tension from my body.

The low, golden light of early dawn touches the window as I awaken. The flat is silent. Tomas lies close beside me, sleeping. I trace the contours of his lips. He smiles in his sleep.

fifteen

THERE IS A MAGICAL BEAUTY ABOUT THE LONG GREEN landscapes of Marinaleda. The fields are close to the river and have been watered. Far in the distance sit the grand villas of the rich who could not be bothered to cultivate the dry land, their opulence testament to their privilege and corruption. The village supplies vegetables to the workers in the villas. In return, the workers tell us of things they have overheard the owners discussing, plans of their own, plans of the government, who is cooperating and who is pretending to cooperate with the government in exchange for free labour, power, and access to important people.

The villagers welcome us. There are several groups and each group has a leader. We are assigned to work the following day. The work is long and hard and at the end of the first day, we are exhausted. There is food and companionship.

"You get used to it," one of the women, Sabina, tells us. "It's good. There's enough for everyone. Nobody goes hungry, and the children are happy and free."

"But what about their education?" I ask.

She smiles. "This is their education. They play, they watch, they learn from nature. We teach them to read and write. When they are older, almost adolescent, they join us.

Each of them has a responsibility. That's important. It makes them feel a part of the community, not outside of it. And you, do you have children?"

I hesitate. I think of Estella and wonder where she is, since she left for England with Seamus. Instinctively, my hand strokes my belly. Something is happening to my body, and I wonder...

Sabina notices the movement. "My dear girl, are you with child?"

I have no answer, blush and turn away.

"For if you are, Angelita, you will need to be assigned to a different kind of work. Something useful, but gentler. Can you cook?"

"I... why yes, of course, I can cook."

"Well? And for many people?"

"I don't know how well, and not for many people, only about six or eight, but people have always liked what I do."

"She's quite a good cook," La Loca tells the doctor. "I think she'd be an asset in the kitchen."

"We must talk to the leader of the group. He will assign you to the kitchen group. You can be of use there, and you won't injure the child with hard labour."

"But I don't know if..."

"If you are really pregnant? We can find out. We have a doctor here."

I'm amazed and grateful at the kindness of people here. They seem to be working towards a common purpose. As time goes on, I will learn what that purpose is, and help to see its realization. I am taken to see the doctor. She is matter of fact and purposeful, but sensitive too.

"Young lady," she says after examining me, "are you with

the father? I mean, not here, obviously, but does he know about this? Is he involved?"

"So… it's true then… I am…"

"With child, yes. You can expect her in about seven months."

"Her?"

"Or him. We don't know that, but all looks well. And about the father…"

"We love each other. He hopes to join me here soon."

La Loca looks at me enquiringly. She will have questions later. I thank the doctor, and we leave.

"Why didn't you tell me?" La Loca demands. "And the father will be joining you? So it isn't Joaquin then, that's for sure. It must be Tomas."

I'm not ready for her usual abrupt approach. "I've only just found out!" I snap. "I didn't know. I thought…"

"Well, you've a lot of thinking to do now, haven't you?" But her voice softens. She puts her arms around me and holds me close. "Listen, my sweet, whatever happens, you know we'll be with you."

"What do you mean, whatever happens?"

"Whether you decide to have the baby, whether you decide to keep it."

"Get away from me! Of course, I'm having the baby. Of course, I'm keeping it! I thought you were my friend! Oh, I wish Tomas was here!" I feel as if I'm about to burst into tears and move quickly away. La Loca follows. "Don't say any more," I implore. "I just need to be alone for a while. I don't need to be forced into decisions, and I don't want to talk about it anymore." She links her arm in mine and walks beside me in silence. We reach the rooms where we're staying, and I go straight to mine. I hear La Loca moving about in the kitchen we share with everyone, and the murmuring low sound of voices, the clatter of dishes. I crawl under the blankets and fall asleep.

The sun is high. I've been asleep several hours. I glance through the window. Not a cloud in the sky, but on the horizon, a rumbling noise as of guns or thunder and a grey moving line. On a table by the bed is a glass of milk, still warm. I sit up, feel the warmth moving through me as I sip, and although it is high summer, the warmth of the milk comforts me. I sigh, pick up my pad and begin to write. The sun is fading when I finish, the distant long grey line has vanished, a dying light sinks below the horizon like an enormous glowing pomegranate. It's getting late. La Loca must have put the milk there, but she hasn't come in. I get up and go to look in her room. Empty. In the kitchen, three women are preparing the evening meal for the workers. They look up and smile when I come in.

"La Loca?" I say.

"Gone."

My heart lurches. "Gone?"

"To Madrid. She'll be back day after tomorrow. Want some dinner?"

I realize I'm hungry, nod and sit down. I wolf down a bowl of vegetable and bean stew and ask for more.

"That's a healthy appetite," Sabina observes between mouthfuls. "There's plenty left. The others will be here for dinner soon."

Does she know, I wonder. Has La Loca told her? I think not. I help wash up the dishes and set the long table for the workers.

"There are oranges," Sabina says, "and coffee if you want some. You look tired. Maybe you should go and lie down. You can have some later."

I nod, smile my thanks, and go to my room. But I'm not physically tired. I am low in spirits and not used to being alone. I'm used to the power and energy of the group, the music, the movement, the work we do together.

I pick up my pad and read. None of it makes any sense to me. They are words that come not from the need to write or say something, but from habit, and they sound empty to me. All my friends have gone. Joaquin is ill, perhaps dying. Seamus is on his way to England with Estella, perhaps there already. Tomas is in Madrid. La Loca is on her way there. I have never felt this alone in my life. But being alone in nature or surrounded by people you know even if you don't care about them and mean nothing to them, is a different kind of aloneness. It's a chosen solitude. This is a feeling of isolation, disconnection from what matters to me. To a person driven by passion and belief there is nothing so enfeebling as when the belief fades, the passion to lie dormant in a fevered mind.

Where do I go from here? Do I just wait? I'm not used to indecision, to just waiting. I begin to understand how my father must feel, cut off forever from the woman he loves, alienated from his daughter, reviled and rejected by the powerful now that he has served his purpose. I need to see him as soon as possible, and before the baby is born, to tell him that he is loved, that he is soon to be an *abuelo*. How can I make this happen? Do I have the courage to go from this place of safety into a world fraught with unforeseen and sudden tragedy alone? My self-questioning continues into the night. In the middle of that night, I hear a voice, an inner voice that has driven me from early childhood. I listen, and in the dim light of early dawn, I pick up my pad and write.

sixteen

I WISH I HAD A PIANO, EVEN AN OLD ONE LIKE THE ONE we found for Estella in Madrid. I write until half into the morning and fall asleep. Now it is time to put the songs to music. I sing, staring out of the window at the distant pastures.

Green and grey/pastures of the lost, the unforgiven/ blending in a distant hope/ longing for a vibrant life/free from pain/from torture/the blind leading the blind/ to an unknown place of safety/as bombs drop on children/on women bearing new life/ohhhhhh, grey and green/ and red/the pastures of the lost.

Three women stand at the door. One is weeping. A young, fragile one smiles. The other turns away.

"Back to work!" Sabina says. "There'll be hungry people here soon!"

The women back out of the room. I respect and admire Sabina, her directness, the hold she has on the present, her work ethic and belief that what she is doing matters. She turns back quickly at the door.

"Nice voice," she says and leaves abruptly.

La Loca has been gone two days. I have not forgotten what she means to me, what she represents, what we have shared: the bombing on the coast, the saving of the child, flight to Tomas and safety in the mountains, the passion, music, love and creativity that have led us to this place.

Tomas. My first love. I try to picture his face when I tell him: love, joy, tenderness, pride. Tomas.

On the third day after La Loca left, I am working in the kitchen, preparing the meal for the workers that afternoon. The door opens, and La Loca walks in, behind her, Tomas. I fling my arms around her and look over her shoulder at Tomas. He smiles, looks down. Something in his face…

"What is it?" I ask. He shakes his head. "I have to work now. Let's talk later. You can wait in my room, over there."

He kisses me gently and leaves. La Loca follows him. I finish the work and head for my room. Tomas jumps up as I come in.

"I've missed you so much," I tell him.

"I can't begin to describe—"

"You don't have to. It's written all over your face. The baby."

"Yes," he says quietly.

"You look worried. Don't be. I am well, even better since you arrived."

He puts his arms around me. "I will help you," he says.

"I know, *carino*, you will help us both. You, me, the baby. I think it's going to be a little girl."

"That's what I want to talk to you about, Angelita." He sits. "Sit here beside me. No, La Loca, you can stay."

La Loca shakes her head. "No. See you later." She closes the door quietly. Tomas avoids my eyes.

"What is it, *mi amor*? What's wrong?"

"Angelita, we cannot have a child now. How can we bring a human being into the world as we know it? It would be cruel." He pauses. "I know a place, a good person, a doctor, who will take care of this for you. I will go with you."

I stare, unable at first to take in what he is saying. I have only one thing to say. "You will be a father, Tomas, whether you agree or not. Nothing can change that."

"Angelita, please…"

"If you love me…"

"I do love you! You are everything to me! I have loved you from the first moment we met all those years ago at the pond, when we were still children… but… now…"

"I won't kill my child, Tomas. Not for you, not for anyone. I want this child."

"I'm begging you, Angelita! Think of all the work we have to do. All we have planned together—"

"I will have our child. *Our* child, Tomas, yours and mine—"

"Darling, I can't let you—"

"Then I am alone. I don't need your 'help.' I'll do all I can to keep this child safe—with or without you."

"But I love you. Angelita, listen to me…"

"The decision is made. The baby will be born. With or without your agreement." I leave Tomas sitting there, leave the room to join La Loca.

She says nothing, just sits silently waiting for me to speak.

"He does not want the child," I say. "I am on my own in this."

"I know. But you are not alone in this, I am here, I am with you all the way. But I have one thing to ask of you." I wait for her to continue. "Could you, would you, consider finishing the next performance we have planned? Just this one. We've practiced. It is nearly ready. It would bring all of us together one last time. You're in the early stages, and if you feel well enough, we could do it."

"Yes."

"That's it? Yes, just like that! Do you need time to think this over?"

"You say 'one last time,' as if we're all about to die. But we're alive, there's new life on the way, and we're going to do marvelous things together. I've already written the songs. So yes, we'll go ahead with the next performance, all of us, Tomas as well, if he wants to, and I hope he does. There may be time for another performance as well, we'll have to see. It could be after the baby comes. She… or he… can be part of it."

La Loca is ecstatic. "Tomas will want to be part of it, I'm sure, Angelita. He wants the best for you, my friend. He's just worried about how the two of you will be able to cope with a baby."

"I understand that, La Loca. But if we were together on this, we could make a difference for all of us."

"He is with you, darling. He loves you."

"Well, I've made my decision. The baby is not negotiable. He'll have to accept that if he wants to be with me."

"He will. I'm sure of it."

"I love him, La Loca, I want him in my life, I've loved him since we were both children back in the mountains. He will be a wonderful father, I know that. I think he'll change when he sees the baby. If he doesn't, then his choice will be to live without us."

"That's not going to happen," she laughs. "I'm as sure of that as I'm sure that Seamus is a courageous, incorrigible, irritating, clever bastard, and that he'll be back, and I love him. Just as you love Tomas. Give him time."

I am grateful for La Loca's directness and love. I need that, for if I'm honest, Tomas's reactions have stunned and hurt me. The thought of getting on with our work is a bright star in a dark, uncertain universe. The realization that I am not alone makes my spirits soar.

I want to begin work again with the group as soon as possible, but Seamus is missing, and we need him, his energy and inventiveness. I have no idea how long he will be gone in England and Ireland, although I'm certain he won't want to stay there and that he'll be back. In the meantime, I feel an urge to get on with preparations for our next work. Where, for example? Joaquin is out of the picture for the foreseeable future, so we have lost his valuable preparatory work on locations and important contacts in government. We must find another way. That way is hidden to me. I see no way of moving forward, finding safe possible locations, contacting important people. I spend sleepless nights wracking my brain, trying to come up with viable plans. Tomas has become inexplicably remote with me. It's as if his mind is elsewhere, and he's unable to express his feelings in the way we have always been able to, forthright and affectionate. I remember La Loca's advice to give him time. I wait.

I try to work out how we can continue with our work. We have the ideas, we have the people, but we are stuck without a safe place to perform, and to whom. It was while I was walking near the city suburbs that something changed. I sat on a park bench, sheltered from the summer heat by the shade of an overhanging jacaranda tree. Three young soldiers walked by. They nodded, and one raised his hand in salute. The gesture was familiar. As they walked on, I sat thinking, remembering. The signal of his hand was unmistakably *No Pasaran*—they shall not pass, the vow of freedom fighters to vanquish the government. I leapt to my feet and walked quickly back to the house, careful to take the back streets.

"What's up?" La Loca demanded as I flopped down at the table and wrote. "You look as if you've seen a vision."

"*Los soldados*," I said. "We have to take it to the soldiers."

"What are you talking about?"

"Not just the soldiers, but their captains, their commanders. They need support, encouragement, a reason to go on. We can give them that. And... possibly... just possibly... some from the other side."

Tomas has been listening intently. "The soldiers already have a reason to go on. That's why they are fighting, and that's what the international brigades are doing here. People from all over the world have come to fight the fascists."

"Do you have a better idea?" I ask tersely.

"We can find another way," he insisted. "It would be dangerous for you, Angelita."

"Just being near Madrid is dangerous," I retorted. "We'll need you, Tomas, and Seamus when he comes back—"

"I'm leaving," Tomas says abruptly. "I'm going home."

"What!"

The words tumbled out as though a dam had been released. "My father was killed on a visit to a town down in the valley while he was trying to send a message to me as the local *correos*. The *fascistas* found the message. They tortured him, burned him alive and strung him up as a warning to others." He flopped down at the table, head in his hands. I exchange glances with La Loca, stunned by his tragic news and trembling at the thought of my own impending loss.

"My mother and sisters are alone. They have nobody to help or protect them. I must go back."

I put my arms around him, hold him close. "I'm so very sorry, Tomas. How... how did you find out?" I whisper.

"My cousin. He didn't want to risk a written message. He got here part of the way on the train from Malaga, the rest of the way by cart. He says they are desperate. They need help with the cow, the land, everything... my mother is not well..."

"Where is he staying?"

"He's already gone back to the mountains. He stayed with a friend on the outskirts, but he had to be careful and needed to get back to his own family."

I try to still the mounting panic I feel. "I see that you must go, *carino*. Your family needs you." My voice shakes.

"Come with me, Angelita. Please! We can both help, and we'll be together."

For a moment, my heart soars at the thought of the peace such a decision would bring to me, to us. But he does not mention the baby or my decision. The issue creates a barrier between us that seems insurmountable. I press my face into his chest, choking back a sob.

"I have something to finish here, Tomas. My love, I cannot go with you."

"You would be safe there, darling. I'm begging you, Angelita."

"It is not near my time yet. When it is, or when it's over, I shall come to you."

"But how? How will you manage? There is so much to do..."

"Seamus will be back soon. He will help."

"I don't want to leave you, Angelita."

"But you will." There is a throbbing in my heart, my hands shake. I will myself to stay calm. I turn away towards our room. "I will help you to pack, *carino*. You will need food and water for the journey." I stop suddenly, deep in thought. "How will you get there? It will be risky."

"I know how to travel. I will be careful."

That night, as we lie together, there is sadness in our gentle touching, as though we are already whispering farewell.

seventeen

Tomas has gone. I throw myself into the work with maniacal urgency, partly to get it done, but mainly to deaden the pain of loss. I feel lonely. It's as if some vital inner part of me has been removed and that space cannot be filled, not by memory, or will, or the need to survive. The sense of emptiness without Tomas has become part of my life. Not even the child can fill the void. But I feel a deep yearning to bring my baby safely home. It is this need that drives me forward now. There are now two things I must do: see my father and write my song. Writing strengthens me. Singing gives me courage.

We still have no word from Seamus, no hint that he has arrived in England or when he will be back. I throw myself into the work.

This is my song/to those who long/ for freedom/a touch of mercy/for hearts and souls in pain/I say again/be free/for it begins with me/Be true/for it begins with you/Out in the dark/a tiny moving glow will let you know/the freedom bird/ the freedom bird/is flying above the fields of home/and you are not alone/This much is true/freedom on earth begins with you.

La Loca listens as I sing the words, nods and dances to the rhythm of the music. I watch her move and know we have much work ahead of us.

*

I stand at the door of my father's house and knock gently, three taps followed by three taps, then two. Our signal. There is movement behind the door, a fumbling at the latch. Something falls. I wish now that I still had my key.

"Papa, are you there? It's Angelita," I say softly. I hear a scuffling sound, a groan, and the door opens. My father stands leaning against the wall, breathing deeply and smiling, his lips a twist of pain. One crutch is on the floor, and I reach down to retrieve it for him.

"Come in, darling, come in," he says breathlessly. "Let's have some coffee." He turns away towards the kitchen. I put my arm around him and guide him to the salon. When he is safely seated, I move towards the kitchen.

"Strong, as always?" I call carelessly over my shoulder to hide the alarm I feel at the sight of his weakness and pain.

"As always," he responds. I lean on the table, devastated by what I've seen, the sturdy, agile father I have known all my life crippled and riddled with pain. My heart aches for him. I finish making the coffee and go to sit beside him in the salon.

"Papa, darling, I am so sorry."

"No pity, Angelita. It demeans me."

"It isn't pity I feel, Papa." I take his hand. "I didn't know, Papy, I didn't know. I just read your papers and drew my own conclusion. Forgive me, Papa, for the suffering I must have caused you. I know what you have done, what you have gone through just to keep me safe." I lift his hand and kiss it and go on holding it as I look into his eyes. "I love you, Papa. I need you. Please forgive me."

He is silent. The clouded, intense blue of his eyes make me think of an impending storm, but he is calm. "There is nothing to forgive, darling. You are everything to me, the reason for living, for going on."

"I have news for you, dear Papa," I tell him. I move closer, holding both his hands. "You will be an *abuelo* before the year is out." His eyes grow large.

"You are telling me…"

"Yes, I am with child."

"And the father?"

"We love each other."

He looks closely at me. "There is something you are not saying."

"He is concerned, thinks I should not work so hard, that I should go with him, but he is happy for me."

"Go with him? Where is he? Is he not happy about the child?"

"He has had to leave Madrid, to go back to the mountains to be with his family. His father was killed, and his mother is unwell. He is the only man left. His family need him."

"And *you* need him, Angelita." His face is troubled.

"Please, Papy, be happy for me, for us. Yes, of course I need him, I love him and he loves me… but there are things—"

"Will he be back?"

"Yes… I… I don't know when… but…" I tremble, remembering that Tomas will not be back, not soon. My father does not reply and becomes very quiet. His hand has stopped trembling, he sits upright holding tight to the arms of the chair.

"I will take you there."

"Take me where?"

"To the mountains. You were happy there. I will go with you. I still have ways and means, I can get transportation, protection."

"Dear Papa. I love you so much. But I must stay in Madrid. I have work to do here. When the work is done, and the baby is born, then, and only then, can I make that decision."

"But your health…"

"I am strong and well. I have a doctor who watches over me. You need not worry, Papa, on that score. But there is something else. I want you to come and live with me… with us… in Marinaleda. You have heard of it, I'm sure."

"Marinaleda! A village not far from Madrid, run by the people—a communist village. Yes, I've heard of it, of course, and it is dangerous for you."

I smile. "It is one of the safest places I have ever been, Papy. The landowners abandoned the fallow land to the people, and they have brought it back to life. Everyone works, all are paid the same wage, and any spare food is shared with the hungry of nearby villages."

"But the government…"

"The government is too busy bombing other places to notice one small village on land belonging to the aristocrats. They are interested only in snuffing out the loudest, fiercest opposition."

"I want to be near you, *hija,* but I'm afraid for your safety, and because of my age, my health, I'm at risk now wherever I am. And you… you are carrying new life, my grandson."

"Granddaughter, I think. I've a feeling it will be a girl."

"Stay here with me tonight, Angelita, and let me think this over. If it is the right thing to do, we will leave in the morning. I can find transportation…"

"It is decidedly the right thing to do. Papa, you cannot stay here alone. If you are with me, I can take care of you."

"Stay with me."

"I will stay tonight, but tomorrow we must leave. I need to get back. There is much work to do."

"Who else is with you in Marinaleda?"

"La Loca—you have met her—she is *Gitana,* a dancer. And Seamus, the Irishman I told you about before. He should be back soon."

"Back? Where has *he* gone? There seems to be an awful lot of coming and going."

"He took Joaquin's little girl to England to be with her aunt there, to be safe. Her father is very ill and closely guarded in hospital here."

"But can you trust Joaquin? I know of him, Joaquin Montalban. He is a captain in Franco's army! How did you come to know him? Is he trustworthy?"

"The *junta* murdered his wife some years ago, and his only thought is to keep his daughter safe. His sister in England will see to that."

"But if they know about Joaquin's wife…"

"They know nothing. They don't connect him to her. They are under the impression that his wife abandoned him and the child and fled to England, where she has family."

"I see." But he does not see. His face tells me that he does not believe this. Joaquin's connection with the government is all he knows and his face is like an open book, his doubt and concern for my safety clearly written there.

"Tomorrow," he says quietly. "Let's see what tomorrow brings. Now I must rest."

"Tomorrow, dear Papa, I leave for Marinaleda. Please

come with me, to watch over me, to be with your grandchild."
I know that if I appeal for his help rather than offering mine,
he is more likely to agree.

The night is long, punctuated by my father's groans as he
tries to sleep in the room next to mine. I am focused on
what the coming day will bring, and my father's decision to
accompany me to Marinaleda. Or not.

A dim grey dawn pierces the window. My father is quiet
now, exhausted by pain and the struggle to find rest. I wait.
After a few hours, a golden light surges beyond the window,
and I go to the kitchen to make coffee. This is his morning
ritual, something he has done all his life, coffee strong and
hot, and thick slices of crusty bread. I take the coffee to his
room. He is very still, breathing hoarsely. I place the coffee
on the table beside the bed and watch him. He is old, his
skin like collapsed parchment, colourless. Memories of his
sturdy strength over the years as I grew to womanhood, his
steadfast love and patience, bring tears to my eyes as I watch
his frail figure begin to stir, nose twitching at the aroma of
coffee. His eyes blink open and he smiles, reaches out a hand
towards me. "Angelita."

"Yes, Papa, I'm here." I help him to sit up, pillow behind
him, and hand him the coffee cup. He sips appreciatively,
eyes closed, leaning back.

"I couldn't sleep last night, thinking of your plans."

"I know, Papa."

"I will come with you."

I lean forward to kiss his cheek. "I am glad, Papa. I need
you beside me."

"But I have one condition," he says. I try to anticipate

what he is about to say but am unprepared for what comes next.

"When I die, you must promise to bury me in the mountains where you were born."

I am astonished. He was born here in Madrid, lived his whole life here and also with my mother. "Papa, I don't understand. You have never lived there. Your whole life has been—"

"Here in Madrid, I know. But it was in the mountains of Andalucia that I first saw and fell in love with your mother. I want to be there at the end."

"I will promise you that. But, Papa, do not talk to me of dying! You have a lot of life left in you yet! Where do you think I got my stubborn nature from? From you, of course! And you will cling stubbornly to life, especially if you are with me and the grandchild!"

He smiles. His face takes on the expression of the father I knew of old. "I will make the arrangements," he says, "to get us safely to Marinaleda. I know people I can trust. But what will the people there make of me? They may not accept me, a man who has worked for the government."

"You are my father. They must accept you. Anyway, they know the story of what was done to you, and why." A light comes into his face, he is reassured, and I am glad.

"We leave tomorrow. I need a little time to arrange transport."

My heart melts as I watch him, filled now with purpose and energy as of old.

It was to be a long journey.

eighteen

A VAN ARRIVES TWO DAYS LATER. INSIDE IT ARE TWO seats and a mattress in the back, for my father. The driver is unknown to me, but my father trusts him and assures me they have worked together for many years. He will take us to Marinaleda. We begin the journey just after dawn. It is not far, but we must be vigilant of patrolling Guardia.

"Alberto, this is my daughter, Angelita. You can trust her with anything." We shake hands.

"She looks like you," Alberto says, and my father grins.

"*Dios mio,* I hope not, that would be a hard load to bear." They chuckle together. I see that they have a friendship, that they understand and like each other, and I am reassured.

"I know the way, Alberto, and can help you with the driving if you need to rest," I offer.

Alberto chuckles. "I know Marinaleda, *senorita*, I have been there many times. I have a cousin there."

We finish breakfast and load the van with blankets, clothing for my father, food for the journey, and leave, my father in the back, myself in front with Alberto.

He has a habit of whistling.

"Stop that tuneless noise!" my father shouts from the back.

Alberto goes on whistling. "It can be useful," he says, "in sending signals. If I whistle three times on a down note, get in the back, quickly, and cover yourself up, Angelita. And you, old man, go back to sleep."

There are no delays on the journey. The van is a government van, and we meet only three Guardia on the way out of the city. Within five hours, we begin the approach to Marinaleda. There is a glow in the distance. I sit up in alarm.

"Fire! There is fire in the village!" Alberto makes a swift turn into the woods and stops.

"I can't see that far. What do you see?"

"Bushes burning, or fields, near houses just inside the entrance to the village."

"We must wait."

"I need to go in."

"You can't go in if there is fire, *senorita*. We must wait to find out the cause of the fire, whether there is an accident, or if there has been an attack. I doubt the latter. The village has always been left in peace. But we must be careful."

La Loca is there. She may be in danger, and I want to press on. But I know Alberto is right. We must be cautious and wait. A voice from the back.

"What's going on? Why have we stopped? It's getting late. We have to press on." My father is impatient now that the decision has been made. I need to reassure him. I climb into the back of the van and sit beside him.

"We're nearly there, Papa. There's fire up ahead. We have to stop to work out what is going on before we enter the village." He tries to sit up. "Relax, Papa. We must wait here a short while. When we know it's safe, we'll go in."

I see the familiar loping figure of a man running from the village towards us. Seamus! Soon we'll know what is going on in the village.

"Stay here, Papa, don't move. I will call you if needed." I open the door to the truck and jump out to wait. Seamus leans on the truck, panting.

"Best if you stay in the truck for now," he tells us. "The fire is nearly under control."

I've been thinking of La Loca and breathe a sigh of relief. "How did it happen?" I ask him. "And when did you get back from England? How is Estella? Come on, tell us what's going on."

"I will, if you'll just let me catch my breath." I hand him some water, and he gulps it down. "It's hot in there," he says. "Thirsty work. Yep, I got back only last night. I took the night boat to Santander and managed to get a cart overland most of the way. Some of the way I walked through the mountains, I know the terrain, thanks to the work I did with the forest workers when we first met, Angelita, when you were trying out being a boy. Must say, I like you more as a girl, lass."

"Seamus, I'm glad you're back, my friend. You are needed here. Tomas has gone back home to the mountains—oh, I see you've heard, of course, La Loca told you—and we need help getting the performance going. This time we're taking it to the soldiers."

"So I hear. Is that wise?"

"They are courageous, but many have been lost and they need support and encouragement. We can give them hope, energy to keep going with the revolution."

"But Angelita... the child... call me old fashioned if you like, but a woman has to take care of herself with a baby on the way."

"I am taking care of myself, Seamus. I know what I have to do, and I'm doing it. We're all working together on this.

My father's in the back. He's not strong, but he can help us with some of the information we need."

"Information?"

"Where to go, who to talk to about what we do, who we can trust or not, and how to contact those who can be trusted. He still has good insights and information into the running of the government and those in power around Franco. My father is well known. Not everyone was in favour of what was done to him. They will want to help him."

"That's good news. But first things first. Let's get everything under control in the village. It's best if you wait here until I signal you to come in."

"How did the fire start?"

"Nothing sinister. It started in the kitchens. A new maid was helping there and overturned a vat of oil near the fireplace. It caught alight and spread across the floor to the straw outside and to some of the trees. People panicked, thought it was some kind of attack, but we managed to get things more or less under control."

"More or less?"

"Two houses caught fire. One is still smouldering. We've found shelter for the families nearby. There's plenty of room."

"La Loca?"

"She's a warrior, that woman! Pitched right in organizing water, making sure the children got safely out of the way. Worked like a man."

"Huh, like a man! You think it's only men who know how to work, how to behave in an emergency?" I scoffed. "I thought you knew women better than that, Seamus, especially La Loca!"

"I asked for that, darlin'. Okay, you're right. My God, I've missed her like hell. Only spent two days in Ireland before shipping out."

"And Estella?"

"Happy. She's with her aunt and learning English, smart kid that one. And she has a piano. Getting used to the horrible food, but anyway her aunt cooks Mediterranean. She's writing songs, misses Spain and her father, but she's adapting very quickly to the way of life, the language, the people, thanks to her aunt, a wonderful woman."

I gaze towards the village as Seamus rambles on. The fire is receding. "Time to go in now? It looks safe enough."

"Right, let's go." Seamus climbs up beside us, and Alberto drives towards the village. "I'm glad to be back," Seamus says, "I've missed the work, the feeling of doing something purposeful, making a difference… and… I've missed La Loca. She's so much a part of my life now. I can't be without her."

"You've got it bad," Alberto observes.

"Yep, she's quite a woman. I adore her, and the great thing is, she loves me too."

"Right, enough about romance," I intervene. "Let's get going."

"Angelita," Seamus says quietly, "I'm sorry about Tomas, really sorry. He's a good man, and he belongs here with us, with you."

My heart wrenches at the thought of Tomas. "He's doing what he has to do, going to his family in their time of need. Soon enough we'll be together again." But I don't know that, and my throat chokes on the words. I have no idea when we'll be together again. The distance between us is great, and not just in miles. I long to have him near when the baby comes and am secretly dismayed that he has had to leave when he is so much needed by my side. But I understand about *Gitanos* and the family code of loyalty. I am not yet his family. But I will be… we will be, the baby and me… This I tell myself often, for without belief in a future with Tomas, I cannot go on.

La Loca stands at the entrance to the village, like a sentinel. As we approach, she begins an *alegria*, and my heart soars at the sight of this wonderful woman dancing for joy at the sight of me. It is said that home is where the heart is, and despite my longing for Tomas, I feel I have come home.

We link arms and walk into the village. The truck follows.

"I was worried when I saw the flames," I tell her. "My first thought was that the bastards had found out where I was, where we all were, and were taking revenge. Now that Seamus is back, we can get on with the work. My father can help with the contacts…"

"Your father!" La Loca exclaims.

"Oh yes, he's here with us. He'll stay with us. He's resting in the back of the truck. He took some convincing. He wanted me to stay in Madrid with him."

"Yes, you can be very persuasive," comes a voice from the back of the truck, followed by a chuckle. "A chip off the old block, as they say."

La Loca and Seamus both nod and grin at me affectionately. "Persuasive is an understatement, sir," they call. "She's downright stubborn and a bit of a bully."

The village reeks of ashes, and I am reminded of the forest fire in the mountains when I was working with the woodcutters. Those days seem far away. I feel nostalgia for the simplicity of that life, the companionship between the men, the gruff kindness of the leader, Fat Bastard.

A crow settles at the top of a half-burned tree. I stare at it as it flutters down to stand beside me, pecking the ground for fallen berries. It shows no fear, cocks its head and peers up at me. My affinity with crows goes back to early childhood. Sometimes they would appear at my bedroom window, and each time after their appearance, something changed in my life, usually for the better: a beautiful new horse, an unexpected visit to see my father, a visit from my big brother. Only once did something bad happen. It was on the morning in the village when I poisoned the river and was attacked by the guard.

I awake at dawn next day to an urgent tapping. A flock of crows is at my window, banging their beaks on the glass. I open the window and they fly in, settle on the bed and fasten lustrous eyes on me, heads to one side. I feel a chill in the room and get up to shoo them out and close the window. Only one remains, peering at me intensely as though silently questioning. It struts and pecks beside me now in between glancing up at me. One of the women comes out from the kitchen and shoos it away. It glides back up to perch at the top of the tree, looking down at me. A chill touches my spine, and I shudder.

The cooking is being done in another place while a team cleans up the mess in the kitchen. Alberto and Seamus help my father down from the truck and into his room next to mine. La Loca and Seamus are nowhere to be seen, they are off alone somewhere, making up for lost time. I force myself not to dwell on where Tomas is, what he's doing, my need of him.

"I need to be going," Alberto says.

"So soon?"

"Got to get back to Madrid, other jobs to do there. But I'll have something to eat first." We place food before him and he eats hungrily. Soon he is on his feet and ready to leave. "Dark soon, better be off."

"Thanks for your help, Alberto, we all appreciate it."

"I owe a lot to your father," he mumbles. "Many's the time he's got me out of tricky situations. Goodbye then." And with a quick wave, he's gone.

I take some food up to my father, but he is already asleep. Gently, I place the dish on the little table by the bed and cover him with a blanket, resolving to check on him later.

I sit alone near the kitchen. I am not hungry but know I must eat to maintain my own energy and for the baby. An intense loneliness washes over me like a huge wave on an empty shore, and I feel again a sense of foreboding. I shake my head fiercely to dispel the sensation and glance up to the top of the half-burned tree. The crow has disappeared.

nineteen

EVERYONE IS UP EARLY NEXT DAY, EAGER TO GET TO work. Seamus helps my father down to breakfast. La Loca cleans up part of the kitchen and sits beside me.

"Where do you want to work?" she asks. "It's not too hot. We could work outside, or there's space in my room. We could put in that table over there for you to write at. Problem is you can't set the songs to music."

"I can do the rhythms for you, would that help? I have the notes in my head. They can be done later, when we have a piano."

"What's up?" La Loca asks and sits down beside me. "You feel all right? You look a bit pale."

"Didn't sleep too well last night."

But La Loca knows me well. She knows something is troubling me. "What is it?" she says quietly.

"I can't put it into words, it's a feeling, an... uneasiness... I can't explain it."

"A premonition?"

"No, not like that, not as defined as that. It's just... everything I know seems to be slipping away."

"I trust your intuitions, you've had them before, back there on the coast, remember, after the bombing, you got up and told us we had to move inland, to the mountains, you and me and Maria del Mar after her mother was killed."

"But it's not like that. I can't describe it. It's something in the gut, a feeling."

"Maybe you're just missing Tomas, Angelita. Don't squash down the sadness. I can see it in your eyes. You can talk about it with me."

"That crow."

"Crow?"

"Yes, last night. It just left, vanished, hasn't been back since… it's unusual."

"I remember. You've told me about them in your childhood, the significance you interpret from their visits, but this is a coincidence, nothing more."

"I don't know that. You don't know that. I can only speak from what I feel inside."

"When a woman carries a child, emotions can be unpredictable. They can change, be strong and inexplicable."

"I know that. No, it's not about the baby. I'm happy about the baby. And yes, I do miss Tomas, but it doesn't explain this… this… feeling of *threat*. That's it. I feel threatened, La Loca, and I don't understand why. I love it here, the community, the people. It has nothing to do with being here. I think it has to do with *not* being here."

"But you're not leaving, not yet. We're safe here, Angelita, we can work here, and—"

Seamus appears from the house. "Someone's coming, two trucks. Get inside, until we know who it is. Go now."

We look into the distance, and sure enough, a large truck is approaching the village. We do as Seamus says and go inside to wait.

Within ten minutes the truck pulls up outside the gate to the kitchen garden, and three men approach the house.

One of them is Alberto. We look at each other, puzzled. We are under the impression that he had to return to his work in Madrid, and now he is back already with two other men.

"Back so soon. I wonder what they want." La Loca looks worried. Two of the men approach the door and knock. Alberto hangs back outside the gate and waits. Seamus asks the men what they want.

"We are looking for Bruno de Caballe and his daughter Angelita."

"I have not seen them lately, but I can give them a message."

The men exchange glances. "We have orders to search the house."

"Orders?"

"Captain Joaquin de Montalban has given the order."

"I will need to see your papers and the written order."

One of the men bristles, pushes out his chest and speaks. The other puts a hand on his arm to stop him.

"There is no need to be alarmed, senor. Captain Montalban is now fully recovered and wishes to see them."

"Good. Glad to hear that. I still need to see your papers," Seamus insists quietly.

"We are not mind readers," the belligerent one puts in. "We just have orders to bring them to see him. I'd like to see the girl especially," he smirks. His companion shoots him a warning look.

Seamus looks over at Alberto behind the gate. "Alberto, come and explain procedures to these two," he calls. "Nobody passes without identification, as you know." Alberto hesitates, walks slowly up the path towards them.

"They say the captain wants to see them to make sure they are all right," he says, looking at his feet.

"They say. I see. Tell me, Alberto, how did the captain know they were here in Marinaleda?" Seamus is quietly matter-of-fact, but about him is a tense atmosphere of caution, alert now to something amiss in the attitudes of the men. "I know you, Alberto, but your two friends here are strangers to me." Alberto shifts from foot to foot. "I need to see your orders," Seamus says decisively to the other two men, "before you come any farther. That is the law here."

"Oh, you have laws here?" sniggers the belligerent one, "I thought you were all—"

His companion cuts him off with a snarled *cayate!* "They are in the truck. I'll get them," he says. All three move to the truck and drive off.

"They've gone. But I think it is no longer secure for us here. Alberto must have been under pressure to tell them where we were. We have to get out."

"Get out?" we blurt in unison. "What is going on?"

"I don't know. But those two bastards clearly had no authorization. That's why they left suddenly. I think they're fascist mercenaries. They probably threatened Alberto's family... You would know about that, Bruno," he calls towards the stairs.

"But why would Joaquin...," I begin.

"He wouldn't. We don't even know if he survived. I'd swear those bastards are Falangists though. They're not on our side, that's for sure, and they're too stupid to realize we can see through their act. I hope you had your hand on the trigger at that window, darlin', 'cause anything could've happened," he tells La Loca.

La Loca puts the rifle down. "What are we going to do? Can we not stay here?"

There is a fumbling movement on the stairs and Bruno calls, "What's going on, Angelita? I heard someone say my name."

"Stay there, Papa, I'm coming to help you." I run to the stairs to help my father down to the kitchen. We all sit in silence.

"Well?" Bruno repeats. "Get on with it. I'm old and feeble but I'm not a child. Tell me what's going on. Why do you all look as if you'd swallowed shit?"

"Someone knows we're here, Papa. We have to leave."

"Who? Who knows?" he demands.

"We don't know for sure, but the Falangists are on to us. I think they're mercenaries. I think they threatened Alberto to tell them where we were."

Two women enter the kitchen to begin the evening meal for the workers.

They look enquiringly at the group sitting silently at the long table.

"You must be hungry. Been waiting here long?" they ask. "It'll be about an hour." The women continue chopping up vegetables and preparing the meat. The group sits in silence. La Loca nods towards the stairs and we all get up to leave.

"Don't worry about us. You can go on socializing with us here, my friends. We're too busy to listen anyway."

We smile and thank them, and go upstairs holding carefully onto Bruno, followed by Seamus.

"Right, what's the plan?" Seamus asks when we get to our rooms. "It'd better be soon because I think those cretins will be back."

"We have to leave the village," La Loca says.

I am appalled. "Just like that! What about all the work, all the plans? And where would we go?"

Bruno has been very quiet. "I'll take you," he announces.

"You, Papa? What do you mean? Take us where?"

"The mountains. It's the only place where you can be safe. The only place where you've ever been safe."

"But how would we get there?" Seamus asks. La Loca nods.

"*Si, senor,* it is a very long journey, and—"

"I can arrange it. I told you I have connections still. I can make it happen. Does anyone have a better idea? I know these people, not them, but the type that were just here. They'll do anything for gain. We have to go."

"But how can we all do this, the long trip, your health, senor, and Angelita… the baby, the long journey."

"Let him speak," Seamus says. "He knows the length of the journey and how difficult it would be, but he also knows how these people think. And he does still have connections in government, those who know him well."

"Will you all stop talking about me as if I'm not here!" Bruno protests. "I am still in charge of my senses, you know, even if my body's giving out. You just need to listen. Then decide. I am not forcing you into this. I just think it is the best thing to do."

We all look at each other. I place my hand on his arm. "We are listening, Papa. Please continue."

"First of all, are you sure you want to leave this place? All of you?"

"Of course…," begin La Loca and Seamus.

"I… I'm undecided," I interrupt. "The situation here is not clear. We need to know where those men got their orders, and then—"

"But, darling, no matter what, you'll be safer in the

mountains, I can see to that," my father says. "And you'll be with Tomas."

"I know that, Papa, but there's more than my safety to think about. There's our work. Our work is also important. And we need to be together to do it. We can't just take off to do what's best for us, when there's so much to do here."

"You can do your work anywhere, surely."

"The preparations, yes, of course. That's no problem, but the end result, the performances, those we have to all do together, no other option. Look, let's think about this overnight, talk more tomorrow, then decide."

Very early the next morning, there is a knock on the door below. I run quickly to answer but stand first behind the door, listening to be sure the mercenaries have not returned.

"Are you there, Angelita?" a familiar voice says. I open the door and fling my arms around Joaquin's neck.

"My dear, it is so good to see you," I tell him. "Come in. All the others are still asleep. Sit down. I'll get some coffee." I notice that he limps a little and carries a stick. "Do you have pain?"

"No, just a small mobility problem caused by the blow to the head. I'm fine otherwise." He gazes fondly at me. "I've missed you, my darling, I heard you had come here." He takes my hand, raises it to his lips. "I have news for you. Estella is in England with my sister, and she's well and happy, but she misses me."

"Yes, I knew she was in England. Seamus took her there."

"And that's not all. I have more news. I'm leaving for England in three days, from Santander, to be with her."

"That's wonderful, Joaquin. Estella will be so happy to see you."

"I've come to take you with me, darling. We can all be together again there and safe in England. There's plenty of room."

I withdraw my hand from his. "I can't do that, Joaquin."

"But, darling, why not? It is not safe for you here. The work you are doing puts you at risk of arrest. In England, you will be safe."

"I am not going with you, Joaquin," I say with finality.

He stares at me, gets up, paces to the other side of the room, returns and sits at the table. "I don't understand. We love each other. We can be together." I turn away. "What is it? What's wrong? I thought you'd be glad to see me!"

"I am glad to see you, Joaquin. I care for you and for Estella. You have been good to me, protected me, cared for me, loved me…"

"I still love you! You must come with me. It's all arranged. We will be together. We will be safe. We can be married there—"

"I am with child," I say abruptly.

He flings his arms around me. "Oh my God, darling, that's wonderful news! We will be married as soon as we arrive in England. We will be a whole family again. I will find work—"

"I'm staying in Spain." There's a pause, a shocked silence, as if I'd cursed.

"But… why?"

"The child is not yours, Joaquin."

The blood drains from his face. He doesn't understand. "What?"

"I said the child is not yours. And I am not coming with you."

He moves away from me, sits in silence, watching me.

"Who?" he says at last. "What have you done? It's Seamus, isn't it? That's why he attacked me, almost killed me, to get me out of the way, so he could go on fucking you! Go on, admit it!" He raises his hand as though to strike me and gets to his feet. "You'll both be sorry for this! I'll see to it."

"Sit down and shut up, or leave." Seamus stands at the foot of the stairs. He has heard everything. "Talk to her like that again, and I'll kill you. No, the baby is not mine and not yours. You have no claim on her. Get out."

La Loca has come to stand behind him.

"It's best you leave, Joaquin. She's not going with you."

Joaquin's face is suffused with rage. He backs out of the room and slams the door. "I'll see you in prison, the lot of you, and I'll be there to see you hang, Seamus, you bastard!"

We hear a car drive away at speed.

"Well, the decision's made then," Seamus says. "We get out of here and double quick! He won't waste time putting them on to us. I'll pack."

I feel tears coming. "He's a good man, my friends. He has been nothing but kind to me. I brush the tears away, stand up. "But you're right, Seamus. This forces a decision. We don't know when they'll be back. Let's pack."

twenty

M Y FATHER SENDS A MESSENGER TO A TRUSTED colleague, obtains a vehicle, a van with enough space in the back to rest and room for all four of us. His colleague himself brings it, alone, and we take him back to the perimeters of Madrid.

My preoccupations with the work at hand have been set aside. We have no alternative now but to leave, and the safest place I know is with Tomas's family in the high sierra of Andalucia. Seamus is relieved.

"Once you're all settled there, I'll come back and get on with the reason I left Ireland to come here in the first place."

"I'll come back with you," states La Loca.

"We'll see about that," he replies.

"It's decided," she tells him and leaves the room. Seamus is red with frustration and disappointment.

"She's a stubborn one, you know, and that's the truth!"

"Seamus," I tell him gently, "she must be allowed to be herself. Is it not enough that she loves you and wants to be with you? You must let her make her own decisions." He begins to protest. "Oh, I know," I continue, "you love her, you want her to be safe take care of her. Believe me, my friend, she can take care of herself! You can share her life, but you cannot rule her life. I speak from experience."

He listens but is unconvinced. "You're missing the point—"

"Am I? Tell me this, Seamus, which is stronger: your love for La Loca, or your need to control her? Answer that to yourself, and there's your answer."

"I'll think about that."

"And when you do, be honest. Your future with her depends on it." He nods and walks away to be alone.

We leave that same day, before dark, my father in the back, La Loca and me in the front, with Seamus driving. We have water and food for the whole journey stored in the back. We drive all night, stopping only for La Loca to take over, so Seamus can sleep. There is a crescent moon, surrounded by a sprinkled tapestry of stars. As we leave the outskirts of Madrid and ascend the mountains, I am torn between a sense of leaving and a feeling of going home. The unease that I felt earlier still lingers, like a dark finger pointing the way to a yet unknown future. I remember the crows, the aura of warning around them, and shudder. I do not mention the crows again to the others. Only La Loca would understand, for she knows my history, my belief in the supernatural, the power of forces unseen except to those with inner vision. But I am confused. There appears to be a clear path ahead, and yet—

There is a loud bang and the vehicle skews to one side.

"Damn!" Seamus curses from the back. "That's one of the tyres gone! Thank God we've got spares. Right-o, everybody out! Let's get to work fixin' this bloody thing!"

We tumble out half asleep, my father still asleep in the back, comfortably unaware. We pull a spare tyre out of the back door and the equipment to put it on.

Seamus and La Loca work tirelessly, while I keep watch in the woods above the road. The signal will be three owl-hoots if anyone approaches. It takes almost an hour to replace the tyre, but at last we're on the move. My father is still asleep.

We move higher, slowly now as the road narrows, the trees tall and sturdy, the star-sprinkled sky slowly changing as the soft glow of dawn emerges through the trees. I recognize some of the areas where I worked with the woodsmen on my journey towards Madrid dressed as a boy. A few fallen trees still lie unlogged, familiar spaces appear where camps were made. It seems so long ago now, so much has happened in between. Our work against the fascists has not come to fruition yet, but I should be happy. I have my father with me at last; soon I will give birth to Tomas's and my little girl; and I am on my way home.

Home.

Why does the word bring so many conflicting emotions in me? A mixture of elation, excitement and an inexplicable feeling of dread. I shake the feelings away as we stop briefly to relieve La Loca on the driving. She tumbles into the back and Seamus sits beside me.

"Let me know when you've had enough, girl," he offers and sits back to snooze. I peer into the lightening gloom and in the shadows beneath the trees. I think I see movement. A deer? An eagle owl ready to surge from the undergrowth? A man steps into the road and raises both hands, as though in surrender. I brake abruptly, and Seamus jerks upright.

"What's up?"

"Someone up ahead."

"Don't stop. Keep driving."

"He has his hands up and no gun. I can't run him over."

"Stop here. Now!" Seamus jumps out and runs for cover of the trees, gun in hand.

La Loca climbs into the cab. "What's going on?"

"A man up ahead. His hands are up. Seamus told me to wait."

"Be careful. It could be—" A sound of gunshot, Seamus rushes from the undergrowth and jumps into the truck.

"Ambush! Move! Fast! GO!"

I cram my foot on the accelerator too late. A large log falls across the path, and we screech to a stop. Two men emerge from the woods. One is Joaquin, the other a large man in uniform. Seamus aims at the man in uniform, who swiftly trains his rifle on me.

"Throw the gun or she dies! Get out of the truck! On the ground!"

Seamus throws the gun and tumbles out. The man ties his hands behind him. "Out, both of you!" the man shouts at La Loca and me. Her rifle is on the seat, but there's no time to use it.

Joaquin comes forward and ties La Loca up. The big man kicks Seamus in the ribs. "Stay there and you live. Move and you're finished!" he growls. "I could finish you now!" He looks questioningly at Joaquin, who shakes his head.

"That's not what I paid you for. Now! Let's go!"

Joaquin lifts me carefully from the ground. The big man runs back up the track, and a small jeep appears. Joaquin lifts me into it. We leave the others on the ground and race off, bumping across logs.

"Don't worry, you won't get far, you fuckers!" I hear Seamus curse in English, but they don't hear or understand him. Soon they are out of sight, Seamus and La Loca still sprawled on the ground. No movement from my father.

We travel at speed for about an hour. The thought of La Loca and Seamus lying on the road behind us fills me with panic. How will they survive? And who will take care of my father, alone and vulnerable in the van? Furious, disgusted, I shake off Joaquin's arm and glare at him.

"Why?"

"Angelita, there was no other way. I had to get you away from those people."

"*Those people?* They are my friends, and I love them. We trust each other—"

"Trust? You trust a man who almost killed me, who would have left me for dead if it hadn't been for you and that woman."

I am furious now. "That woman, as you call her, has more courage in her little finger than you have in your whole body. You have no idea what she has gone through, what she has lost and suffered, yet she is still determined to carry on, to rally the International Brigadiers and others against your evil boss!"

"My *boss*? You know that is not true. You know I'm fleeing to England to be with Estella, and you know that you're with me now because I love you! We are no longer safe while Franco is in power. Why do you think I'm taking you to England!"

"Against my will," I say bitterly.

"But, Angelita, the baby, Estella, a new life far from here where we'll all be safe."

"I don't love you. I don't want to go."

"You have no choice now. I love you, and I'm going to take care of you."

"There is always a choice. *Always.* And if you truly loved me, you would allow me that choice."

"You will see, darling, when we are in England with Estella and safe. You can still work on your music. My sister has a piano. She is a nurse and can help to take care of you when the baby is born."

"You're deluded, Joaquin, and you are ruining anything that was left between us. Oh yes, I have cared for you. You've been good to me when I needed it most. But I am not in love with you. You must not do this. It is wrong."

"Wrong? Wrong to protect the person I love? You've changed, Angelita. You're not the young woman I first met."

"No, I'm not, and you are right. I have changed, I'll do everything I can to bring down this corrupt regime, and that means taking risks, risks you are clearly not prepared to take, and that's why you're fleeing."

"But the child—"

"She will grow up in a world where women make their own decisions, where they have choice or justice, where they will be partnered with their men, not subjugated and denied the right to be free to carve their own destiny."

"And do you think I don't I care about my own daughter? Answer me that! You know how I adore Estella, will do anything to protect her. That's why I agreed to let her stay in England after your friend took her there. So that she can be free. That's why I'm joining her there."

"You talk of freedom? That's ironic, considering what you are doing to me now! You are forcing me, forcing me to leave here against my will!"

"Because I love you, Angelita! Because I know this is best for you."

I feel the heat of rage building in me and force myself to remain calm.

"Best for me, or for you? You can never ever force me to love you. Each minute that passes, I like you less for what you are doing, and for your cowardice. This is really all about you. Well, I tell you now, I will make sure my child knows that you are not her father, and I'll tell her what you have done here. One day, I will tell Estella too."

The blood drains from Joaquin's face. "Leave Estella out of it!" He turns to his adjutant. "Let's get going. Put her in the jeep. We'll soon be through these woods and on our way to Santander."

I am shoved none too gently into the back of the jeep, and we bump off through the woods. We have been driving for several hours before light fades behind the tall trees around us. The driver brakes suddenly. "There's a deep hole in the road ahead, we must make our way around it." He edges carefully around the pit.

A tall, bulky figure emerges from the woods. I stare through the front of the jeep as a large figure comes towards us.

"Yes, it's deep," he nods. "Took quite a long time. You'll have to get down and help fill it up. There's no way around the side of it."

I recognize the voice, the deep chest-rumble. Fat Bastard! But how could he have known? Then I recall Seamus's curse as we left. *You won't get far, you bastards!*

Seamus has set this up. Seamus, dear unpredictable ingenuous Seamus, who always has a plan, who never leaves anything to fate! I want to shriek for joy, but stay silent, my heart pounding. Joaquin's guard points his rifle. From the forest, six woodsmen emerge and stand behind Fat Bastard, who is now holding his axe above his head. It's a signal. The six woodsmen move to surround the jeep, axes swinging.

"I'd throw the rifle down if I were you," Fat Bastard rumbles, "and let the girl out."

"Do as he says," Joaquin orders the adjutant. "These men are ruthless."

The rifle is tossed to the ground. I slide out the back of the jeep and cross to the big man, bury my face in his enormous chest.

"Get behind me, girl-boy," he chuckles. "Must say, I like you best this way. Always did think you were a bit slender back there in the mountains, skimming up trees like a little spider."

"Don't hurt him," I whisper.

The men work swiftly to fill the hole.

"Get out of here," Fat Bastard growls to the two men by the jeep. "And I'd go quickly if I were you."

Joaquin gazes at me, horrified. "Are you staying with these louts? Say something!"

"These louts?" I laugh. "These louts are twice the man you could ever be. Goodbye, Joaquin. Give my love to Estella." I stand behind Fat Bastard and watch the jeep drive off swiftly. A battered truck bumps from between the trees. Fat Bastard and one of the woodsmen get in.

"Get in, girl. We've a bit of backtracking to do before dark. See you later, lads," he calls back to the men.

twenty-one

IT TAKES US SEVERAL BUMPY HOURS TO REACH THE place where we had been ambushed. To my amazement, my father sits on a log close to La Loca and Seamus, methodically sawing through their bonds with a sharp knife.

"Papa! How did you get down from the truck? And where did you get that knife?"

"Never travel without one," he grins, turning to the other two. "Sorry it took me so long, kids. I was fast asleep. Still would be if it hadn't been for that damned eagle owl in the woods right near the truck. Scared me half to death with its great surging wings."

"No need to tell me how you got away," Seamus says. "You were right on time, Fat Bastard. So, did you let him go?"

"There was no point in hurting them," I tell him. "Joaquin is on his way to be with his daughter. That's all I care about. She needs him. Seamus, how the hell did you manage to set it up?"

"Oh, Fat Bastard and me have been in touch one way or another ever since we worked together in the woods, haven't we, mate? All bark and no bite, and he'll do anything for you, lass, ever since your little experiment with boyhood in the mountains on the way to Madrid. Quite the little tree-skimmer, I hear."

"I'd be on the way to Santander and England without the two of you," I laugh, turning to La Loca. "You're right about Seamus, my friend. He is a stubborn bastard, but he does always have a plan—and thank God for that!"

"*Jesus Cristo*, what I'd do for a stiff Irish whisky right now," Seamus says, ignoring me. "Now will ye stop with the groveling thanks and help get La Loca free. There's another knife in the front of the truck."

Fat Bastard pulls his own knife from his belt. "Never travel without one," he quips, grinning at my father.

"We'll leave tomorrow morning early for the mountains," Seamus says. "And for now, you're staying, Fat Bastard, until tomorrow. Tonight, we feed and water you and give thanks for stubborn bastards like you. I know one when I see one, and I was starting to think I was outnumbered here! Mind you," he grins, staring at La Loca and me, "there's some women I know who'd give us a run for our money!"

"And we'd win," La Loca says, hugging him. "Right then, let's get cooking. Cut up the rabbits, Seamus. We'll have a good stew tonight."

"I can't," Fat Bastard says solemnly.

"Whaddya mean, you can't? Can't stay until tomorrow? It's only…" We all protest.

"Can't have rabbit stew. Sorry. Call it stupid if you like. I just can't eat rabbit. I once had a pet rabbit when I was a kid, I called him Floppy Fucker. We were best friends. He came everywhere with me and wrapped himself around my neck when it was cold. Then one day, he disappeared. I looked everywhere, no sign of him. I cried. My mother tried to console me, saying he'd be back soon, that he'd probably found a girl rabbit. But she gave my father a funny look. He said nothing. Nobody told me, not until I was older, that the stew we had the next day had Floppy Fucker in it. I never forgave them. So you see why I can't eat rabbit stew."

Everyone is quiet. Who would have guessed that this big, rugged woodsman, capable of wielding an axe like a warrior, had the heart of a gentle child? I am certain now, that he would have let Joaquin and his sergeant go, rather than hurt them, no matter what they did.

"To tell you the truth," Fat Bastard went on, "I don't really like eating animals at all. I could live on cheeses and vegetables. But I do eat cow and pig if there's nothing else."

"That's good," I tell him, "because we've got lots of cheeses in the back of the truck, if they haven't gone off, and we can get root vegetables and fruits from the woods. In fact, I think we have some apples back there too."

"Let's go picking, then," La Loca says. "I'm starving."

It was a happy night, full of anecdotes, hilarious memories of working in the woods.

"I'll never forget the night I caught her in the woods peeing like a boy," Seamus tells everyone. "I thought she was going to run off. But she stayed, and worked like… a young man… Yea, she really pulled it off. The work I mean. She never pulled her knickers off again after that, unless a long way off."

Seamus has three bottles of Rioja tucked away in the back for a special occasion. By bedtime, we are all well lubricated, sleepy, and don't care where we sleep, so we bed down in the woods with blankets, under bivouacs in case it rains. Papa climbs back to the mattress in the back of the truck. Seamus and La Loca are nowhere to be seen.

We awake just after dawn to sounds of someone moving around and an aroma of coffee. Fat Bastard makes the best coffee I have ever tasted, full bodied like himself, and strong enough to get the laziest, most tired person up and awake. He has laid out a feast of cheeses, rough bread and fruits. We eat slowly, with the sense that something wonderful is coming to an end, and prolong these last moments with Fat Bastard.

"Where will you go from here?" I ask.

"Back to the safe house. The lads will wait for me on the outskirts, just in case of trouble. Three more have joined us, International Brigadiers, one from England, two from Germany."

"I wonder what moves people to come to Spain when it's so dangerous for them, not knowing if they'll live or die," Seamus muses.

"You would know, fool," La Loca says affectionately. "You're Irish."

"Yea, but that's different. All Irish are mad."

"True," she agrees.

"But there again, we know what it is to be punished, tortured, have our identity scorned and removed. That's how the IRA came about, although I don't agree with their methods."

"You refer to the English, of course. Yes. That was war, an invasion."

"Well, while I'd love to stay and participate in your political discourses, I do have to move my arse now." Fat Bastard heaves himself up. "So long, everyone, *hasta la proxima*." So saying, grabs his bag and is swallowed up by the trees. I wonder if I shall see this brave, rude, kind, tower of a man, ever again, and the thought saddens me.

Silence. We are all thinking of the past, looking to the future.

"We should get a move on!" my father calls from the back of the truck. We look at each other, grin, get to our feet, begin clearing everything into the truck.

Moving upwards slowly at first, we breathe in the smell of nature and peace around us, the gift of the tall green trees. For a moment, it is hard to imagine that far below, many people are dying.

twenty-two

THE PEACE IS SOON SHATTERED. AHEAD, HIGHER UP, much higher, come sounds of gunshots. We stop.

"I'll go on ahead." Seamus slings his pack onto his back, shoves in the water sack, and leaves. "Wait for my signal," he calls over his shoulder. Soon he is lost in the upper forests.

We drive the truck into the side of the woods, break off branches to cover the truck as best we can, scatter the ashes of the fire, pile stones and weeds on top, and wait. We are still waiting as the glint of morning sun strokes the treetops. Still no signal from Seamus. After two hours, La Loca becomes restless.

"We have to do something."

"We are doing something," I tell her. "We're waiting."

"I need to do something active…"

"Then go off somewhere and practice your dancing," I snap and immediately regret it. I'm as anxious as she is. I just express it differently.

"Maybe I will," she says, but she stays sitting there, staring up the track white-faced, the tell-tale tapping of her toe signaling her anxiety.

"You love him very much," I say quietly.

She lowers her head, brushes back the strands of thick, shining black hair that make me think of crow's wings.

"Without him in my life now, I don't know where I'd go, what I'd do. Life without him would be bleak, empty, meaningless. I question why I am here at all, what I'm doing, and why."

"You know what you're doing and why."

"Oh yes, the work of course, but he is the missing link in all of this for me. He is what makes me feel alive, gives me courage, the will to go on. I am more creative when I'm near him. He shines a light into the darkness I've lived through, shows me that there is always a way forward."

"Sshh! Listen…" Through the forest drifts the sound of the owl: one, two, one again. "He's on his way back! Let's get ready. Take the branches off."

"Wait!" my father whispers in the back of the truck. "Wait until you are sure."

We wait a few moments more. The call is repeated. Swiftly, we move the branches from the truck and pull out into the road. "Let's go forward to meet him," La Loca says.

"No. We wait here. That's what he told us to do. He has a reason for it. Remember, he always has a plan."

We wait. After five minutes, Seamus appears at the end of the track. "What's keeping you?" he says, irritated. "Did ye not get my signal?"

"We did, but you said to wait here. Don't give conflicting orders," La Loca retorts.

"Come on then, let's be off." He kisses her forehead. "It was just some hunters up ahead, and they're all right. They're with us. They've moved on now, down towards the valleys, but they gave us dinner for the next two days. Rabbits. Just as well Fat Bastard's gone. He'd hate that, big softy." He jumps into the driver's seat, and we continue carefully along the track that has become mountainous, steep and bumpy. We must take care not to break anything, as we have no spare parts.

The terrain and the forest paths look familiar to me. I feel sure it was around here that I left the woodsmen to continue down to Madrid alone. There is a wide crystal stream running along the right-hand side of the track, and I recall the incident with Romero and the mountain girl, how she escaped by jumping into the water, how he grabbed me, cursed me when I broke his nose. But my adventure and imposture with the woodsmen gave me courage and strength. Afterwards, I felt that I was capable of anything and could even kill a man. That discovery has stayed with me, and I now know that I would kill to protect the innocent. As this thought comes to me, I remember my time in the village holding-house, the attack by the guard, and my defence. I still do not know whether he lived. But I can never return to my village until I know.

Soon the track narrows to the point where we have to clear a way through or abandon the truck.

"We have to clear a way," I say. "We cannot abandon the truck. My father could not manage the walk up the mountain."

"We're almost there," Seamus points out. "Just about ten more kilometers."

"It might as well be a hundred," I insist. "No. We have to clear the way through, at least until we're much closer."

Seamus ponders this. "Agreed. When we're much closer, I will carry him."

We hack and widen the track. My father sits on a log, sharpening the axes needed for the task ahead. My heart sings at the thought of home ahead.

Home. It has been said that home is where the heart is.

Darkness falls. Everyone is exhausted from hacking down branches to clear the track, but all of us want to go on, even my father, who peers out from the back of the truck when we stop.

"Can we not keep going?" he asks. "I think it's not far now, is it, Angelita? To the high sierra and the place where Tomas lives?"

"Papa, we all need to rest. We're pushing the limits. We should be there by tomorrow night, but we have to stop now. Everyone's hungry and tired."

He nods in agreement.

We pull into the side of the track. La Loca makes a fire to cook the rabbits and vegetables. "By the time this is over, I don't know how you all feel, but I'll have had enough rabbit stew to last me the rest of my life," she sighs, stirring the large pot.

"I'm off to look for wild asparagus," Seamus announces and disappears into the forest. Two hours later, he has not returned. We have all eaten. Seamus's food sits in the pot on the embers to keep it warm.

"He must be picking a hell of a lot of asparagus," La Loca remarks. But there is tension in her voice. He has been gone too long.

"There are wild strawberries around here," I tell her. "Farther up where the hills are bare and catch the sun. He's probably sitting gorging on them. Just hope he saves some for us." But my casual comments don't match my real feelings. He has been gone too long.

Another hour passes. We decide to make bivouacs to

protect us from the rain that has begun to drip through the thick branches. It is cold this far up, and we lie down, cover ourselves with blankets and pretend to sleep. My father snores peacefully in the back of the truck, but La Loca and I are wide awake. No sign of Seamus.

"I'm going up," she whispers, "to look for him." She grabs her rifle and vanishes into the forest. I feel this is unwise but know better than to argue with her when she has made up her mind. I wait, staring up through the darkened trees, forcing myself to breathe deeply. Sounds. Feet on branches, more than one person. I shoot up and stand by the fire, peering at two figures emerging from the forest. Seamus's hands are tied behind his back, he limps and his face is bleeding. The man pushing him forward looks familiar.

"Romero!" I gasp. "What are you doing? Why are you here? The others have long gone down below back to the city."

"I left that gang long ago," he snarls. "Better off on my own, doing what I like when I like." He pushes Seamus to the ground near the fire and looks me up and down. "You're coming with me, woman. I need some rest and recreation. Someone to touch in the night." He comes close. "You look familiar. Do you have a brother? You look like a boy I worked with in the woods months ago. The little fucker broke my nose." He grabs my arm, his breath on my face fetid and hot. I push him away. He staggers but keeps his feet, launches himself on me and beats my face.

There is a loud crack. He drops to the ground, clutching his stomach and groaning. Another shot. He lies still.

I whirl to see La Loca emerging from the forest, slinging her rifle over her shoulder. She goes over to Romero and pushes him with her foot, kicks his gun away.

"I can't manage Seamus alone. He's bleeding and needs help. It's not far. Let's go. Get that bastard's gun first just in case he comes to and tie him up."

"What happened? No, never mind. I'll go with you. You can tell me on the way."

Seamus was shot in the thigh and arms and pistol whipped about his head.

"He'll be all right," she assures me. "But we have to get him into the truck. There's no way he can carry your Papa now. We'll have to clear the track most of the way to the pond."

"Once we're there, we'll get help. Tomas will come and help to carry them up to the house. But first let's get some food into Seamus, bind the wounds and put him in the back. All of us need to get some sleep. We'll be up at the crack of dawn to work on the track."

We manage to get Seamus up, supporting him between us with some difficulty, for his injuries make him heavy and he staggers, his full weight upon us. We push him bit by bit into the back of the truck and bathe him, tearing an old shirt of La Loca's into strips to bandage the wounds. Gently, we remove his trousers and underpants to get at the thigh wound.

"Never thought I'd object to two women takin' my pants off," he groans. He hasn't lost his sense of humour. We feed him some stew and give him water. La Loca squeezes in beside him. My father is still asleep. I go to the bivouac and cover myself with blankets. Romero is dead. I drag him to the forest fringes and cover him with branches. I lie still at last, the gun beside me. Exhaustion cloaks my mind and limbs. I sleep.

twenty-three

THE NEXT MORNING, I SLEEP UNTIL SUN FILTERS through the trees.

My father slides down from the truck and limps to make the fire and put on coffee. La Loca and Seamus are still asleep. I push off the blankets and go to help my father build a fire. It is cold, the sun obscured by low branches. I light the fire and begin the laborious work of clearing the track. I work for an hour, with little headway, and wish La Loca and Seamus would wake up and help.

As though she'd heard me, La Loca appears from the truck and heads for the coffee.

"You must've been up for hours to get even that much done. It's tough. When Seamus is stronger, he can help."

"I'm stronger," announces a voice from the truck, and Seamus slides down to join us by the fire. "Even stronger after that coffee. Let's have some."

We sit looking at the track, each of us wondering how long it will take, to break through.

"There's another way," Seamus says.

"No, there are no short cuts," I tell him. "I know these woods well. Only that track will take us to the pond. It's not too far."

"There is another way," Seamus repeats. "One of us goes

on ahead and brings back help. With Tomas and the children, and all of us, we can make headway."

I nod. "It's a good idea. But who goes? I know the way best. I should go, and when I get near the pond, I give the signal. Tomas will hear, and he will come immediately." The others look at each other.

"What if something happened, if you needed help… the baby…," Seamus began. "It's not a job for a woman with child."

"I'll go with her," La Loca says. "Just in case anything happens. You two can stay and keep chipping away at the track, you Seamus with your good left arm, and Bruno can sharpen the tools."

"Let's have breakfast and get going then. Hand me the bread."

"Wait a minute," my father intervenes. "I haven't agreed to this, my daughter going off into the mountains."

"It's decided, Papy," I tell him, kissing his cheek to soften the blow of taking the matter out of his hands. "You can't always give the orders, you know."

"Especially with two women like you involved," says Seamus. "That's for darned sure!"

"I'm going to get boots on, and something warm. It's damned cold." La Loca reappears fully dressed and throws a warm jacket and boots at me. "Let's get going!"

"*Si, Capitan,*" I grin, pulling on the boots and jacket. "Put some food and water together for us, Papy, enough for two days. It won't take that long, though."

"How will we know when you're there?"

"I'll howl. It may be too far away to hear, but you'll know all right when we all appear to help with the track. Just be patient, and get on with whatever you can do here."

My father and Seamus look worried as we leave.

The going is tougher than we thought, the ground between the trees rocky and bumpy. It rains late in the afternoon of the first day. We sit under the bivouacs and munch cheese and bread. The downpour increases, and we decide to call it a night. Covered in blankets and close together for warmth, we fall into an exhausted sleep.

Just before dawn, there is a surging in the undergrowth. La Loca leaps to her feet, rifle at the ready.

"Damned eagle owl!" she curses. "Let's not bother to light a fire, just head on. What'd you think?"

"Agreed. Something to eat first, though."

"Oh yes, I forgot you're eating for two. Here, have the rest of the cheese."

Within a few hours, I recognize the terrain. I have been here before with Tomas, hunting and exploring the hills, sometimes on horseback but often on foot. I move forward more urgently, eager to get closer to the pond.

Suddenly, there it is, sparkling in the rising sun like a patch of silver in the clearing. I lift my face to the sky and howl. There is no response. I howl again, once, twice, three times. The third time, there is an answering howl. Tomas has heard. My heart leaps with joy, I build a fire for coffee, put the pot on and sit down with La Loca to wait. Within the hour, Tomas appears at the foot of the mountain leading to his home and stops, sees us and with huge strides, heedless of the bushes and rocks, leaps down the hill towards us, Maria del Mar close behind.

He sweeps me up and cradles me in his arms. I curl my arms around his neck, lay my head on his chest. Softly, he kisses the top of my head and places me gently beside him on the ground by the pond.

"I've waited so long for this," he murmurs. "Wondering if you would come and when, or if you'd stay in Madrid to have the baby. Oh, *carino*, you must never go away again."

Maria del Mar is weeping with joy.

"I have missed you so much, Angelita. I am happy here, but nobody can fill the space left by you. Please don't ever go away again. Promise!"

I take her into my arms and kiss her small wet cheek. "Sweet Maria, you will help me with the new baby when it comes. I promise you this, if I leave again, you will come with me."

Her face changes. It is like watching the sun come through after a night of torrential rain.

I turn to Tomas.

"We all have to go back down, Tomas, to help the others to cut a way through so that we can get the truck up. My father is too frail to make the journey any other way, and Seamus is injured."

Tomas nods, asks no more questions. "We will all go. The children are strong, and they can help us. I will leave Pepita with my mother. She is the eldest and will care for her for a few days. Maria del Mar will also stay with her to help my sister.

"How is she, your mother? Is she recovering?"

He looks downcast. "She is weak. It's a question of making the time she has left comfortable, letting her know she's loved, that we won't abandon her."

I hug him. "We will stay with her as long as she needs us, Tomas, to be sure. We will not return to Madrid until…"

We sit quietly for a time. Tomas looks at us enquiringly. Time to get back to work on the track. I take Tomas's hand. "We must go, *carino,* it is important that we get the truck up here. My father is waiting."

"The other girls will come with us."

Together, we head back down the mountain, La Loca, Tomas, three of the girls, and myself. We take only food and water for the journey, and blankets for the cold. Tomas stays close to me, holds my arm across the rugged terrain. The journey back seems shorter. It is downhill. We are all together and feel powerful in our unity of purpose. As the truck comes into sight at last, the girls run the rest of the way, and immediately work on the track with the implements we have brought from the house. We eat as darkness falls and fall below our bivouacs into an exhausted slumber.

Next morning, we are ready to move on. Seamus starts the engine and moves slowly forward, my father and one of the girls in the back in case he needs anything. La Loca and I take turns riding in the front with Seamus. The others follow on foot behind the truck. Once, we hit a boulder, and everyone heaves it out of the way. No damage done.

At last, the water of the pond glistens through the trees. The girls run towards it and jump in. My heart sings. Home. I feel the baby move gently inside me and sit to rest on the grass beside the pond.

Tomas's eldest sister comes bounding down the hill, white-faced, followed by Maria del Mar. "She's gone," she whispers, flinging herself beside Tomas.

"Gone? What are you saying?"

"Last night she was very tired. When I took her food this morning, she didn't wake up. Mama has gone." Her sobs are heartrending. The other girls come from the pond and cling together close to Tomas.

"We must go and prepare her now," he says. His voice is calm, but his hands are shaking, his eyes wet as he places his arms around the children. "We must go now," he repeats. "Follow when you can," he tells the rest of us and moves stolidly up the mountain to his home without looking back.

People have different ways of dealing with grief, and Tomas retreats silently within himself.

The funeral takes place the following day, as is the custom.

The men carry the coffin to the orchard and place it beneath the trees she loved so much. The headstone has been carved by two Gitano friends, chestnut wood with engraved garlands of roses and a tree to symbolize growth and eternal life. La Loca performs a slow dance around the grave. I stand by the guitarist and sing a soft lament. Wildflowers are thrown onto the coffin as it is lowered to the earth. I hear the soft weeping of the children.

A simple meal has been set in the shade of the trees and is shared in silence except for the chords of the guitar. Tomas tells me later that the quietness was unusual for a Gypsy funeral, which is often accompanied by loud lamentations. But, it was what she would have wanted: peace in her beloved orchard, and the people respected that.

I wonder what to do about my father, since Seamus is hurt and cannot carry him up the mountain to the house. I decide to stay with him in the back of the truck. The night passes slowly. Twice I feel the baby move strongly. She will not be ready to be born for at least another month. I place my father's hand upon my belly to feel the movement. He smiles. I fall asleep, my arm around my father's chest.

I awaken early to sounds of someone moving near the truck. Papa is still asleep. I peer out of the back as Tomas approaches.

"I've brought you some food and some milk. We have two cows now, you know." He helps me down, and we sit together by the pond. He is very quiet.

I sit with my head on his chest, my hand in his.

"I love you, Tomas. I've loved you so long, from when I first saw you naked at the pond, your black hair sparkling in the sun. I wonder if our child will be dark or fair like me."

"She might have black eyes and fair hair."

My father is stirring in the truck.

"We will have to help him up the mountain," I say, "but first, breakfast. Let's help him down." There is no need. He has already slid out of the back.

"I felt the baby move," my father tells Tomas, "last night just before I fell asleep. And I dreamed that she will have black eyes and fair hair and be willful like her mother." We laugh.

"You may be right, Papa."

"Are you to be married?" my father asks Tomas "You seem a good man. That's what you should do."

"It's not the first thing on our minds, Papa." I smile. "We have a lot to do."

"Senor," Tomas says, turning to my father, "we will wed in the *Gitano* way, and very soon. I will arrange it." My father shakes his hand and is pleased.

Tomas is true to his word. He speaks to me about it, and we

agree that since he no longer has parents, the *boda Gitana*, the traditional Gypsy wedding, will not involve the *pedimiento* or *casamiento*, the engagement party and wedding ceremony, and there will be no formal ritual.

"The *panuelo* ritual and the *El Yeli* are somewhat irrelevant, anyway," he says, grinning at me.

"What do they mean?" I ask.

Tomas hugs me. "Well, the *panuelo* is physical proof that the bride is a virgin, and the *El Yeli* is sung to the bride for giving her honour to her husband. We've gone a bit beyond that, don't you think?" He smiles.

I pat my belly and laugh. "You could say that, but at least we'll have our daughter at our wedding, if you see what I mean."

My father has been listening. "I like tradition," he tells us. "Can we not at least have some of your traditions?"

"Yes, indeed! I have *Gitano* friends farther down the mountain. They will organize a party for us. We will have music, singing, and dancing. And we will have the tradition of the eating of the bread."

"What is that?"

"Both the bride and groom each take a piece of bread and place a drop of their blood on it; they then eat each other's bread."

"I like that," Papy says, "the music, the singing and dancing, the ritual of the bread. It will be a good party."

"I'm so happy you're here with me, Papy. Do you not love it here, the animals, the birds, and being at peace with the world?"

"What makes me happy, darling, is that you are safe, that you have joy in your life, it's all I've ever wanted. I will stay with you here."

Tomas sits on one side, my father on the other. The baby is moving vigorously and I place their hands on my belly.

I feel loved.

twenty-four

THE ENERGY AND JOY OF THE *BODA GITANA* IS something I have never experienced, and I'm enchanted. We are joined by *Gitano* friends from farther down the mountain, people who have known Tomas's parents and grandparents for years.

I am brought in on a round platform festooned with bougainvillea and wildflowers and placed in the centre of the garden. Dancers appear in bright red and blue flamenco dresses, the men in short black jackets and high shoes, and dance around me to the music of three guitarists playing bulerias, a swift and whirling joyful rhythm.

The simple ceremony of the eating of the bread, each with a drop of blood, follows. The symbolism is powerful. There is silence.

La Loca performs a dance of her own invention. The people watch in wonder, using "palmas," the rhythmic clapping of the hands, faster and faster until she ends with a bow and a flourish in front of us.

The girls have prepared a meal of roasted pig, breads, fruits, cakes and homemade wines. The feasting and music last for three days.

Tomas has built a little house for the two of us not too far from the main house where my father, La Loca and Seamus, and the children live.

I sense a restlessness from La Loca and Seamus. They are not unhappy here. I know they love the place, but they are restless. The have never stopped planning and dancing, playing my songs and singing. It comes as no surprise to me when, just as the sun goes down on the last day of their first month with us, there is a knock on the door of our little house. La Loca and Seamus stand there, and I welcome them in.

"I'll be brief and to the point," La Loca begins.

"As always, dear friend."

"We have to go. We love it here, but we need to move on."

"I get it. You need to work again. I understand. I'm sad to see you leave, but I have been expecting it. Dear friends, it won't be too long before I join you. It looks like the war is coming to an end, but with Franco still in power, there's still much to be done. When are you thinking of going?"

"Tomorrow."

I'm dismayed. "So soon! You won't see the baby."

"We'll be back, Angelita. Be sure of that, and probably before you are ready to come and join us. And we will see the baby, carino, Whether you follow us or not, we will be back."

A sense of loss assails me. I feel faint. It's as if an energy has left my body, something essential to my power is fading away. I shake the feeling off.

"I have something for you, something you must keep and use. Treasure it, until we meet again." I go into our bedroom and from a small cupboard by the window, take out a packet of papers. I hand them to La Loca. "My songs. All of them.

Take them with you. Someone else can sing them if need be, but I will need them myself when I join you again."

Tomas shifts uneasily beside me. "Angelita, should you not keep them until you are ready to sing them yourself? I know you will want to. There are years of your work there. One day you will need them."

"I trust La Loca to do the right thing, the only thing, and that is, to share the messages in the songs."

La Loca is visibly moved. She takes the packet from me and turns away. "No goodbyes," she says, her voice muffled. "*Hasta la proxima*". Until we meet again. Seamus follows her out the door.

"How can we use them?" I hear Seamus say. They don't belong to us."

"We will find a way."

"Wait!" I call after them. I reach into the pouch around my neck that holds the golden disc Tomas gave me, made by his grandmother from gold found in the rivers years ago, a talisman, for protection, he told me. I look into Tomas's eyes, hold up the disc and signal with my head towards La Loca. He nods.

I press the disc into La Loca's palm.

"My song for you. Never let it go," I tell her.

La Loca presses the disc to her lips. It shines in the golden light of evening. She turns it over to read the inscription.

"*Libertad*."

When they leave and Tomas has gone to help his sisters, I walk to the orchard and stretch out in the shade of an apple tree. The leaves and grass are cool on my back.

The baby moves as I place my hand on my belly. I fall

asleep. When I awaken, I gaze up at the gently falling leaves. There is a rhythm in their silence and in my head, sounds form. A leaf touches my cheek, and I breathe in the sweet scent. An apple falls on the ground beside me. It is pink and white and round like the face of a small child. I reach and bite into it. It is crisp and sweet.

bibliography

John Hooper, "The New Spaniards" 1995

Giles Tremlett, "Ghosts of Spain" 1979

Laurie Lee, "A Rose for Winter" 1955

Joan Fallon, "Daughters of Spain" 2009

Ronald Fraser, "Blood of Spain" 1979

Stuart Christie, "General Franco Made Me a Terrorist" 1964

George Orwell, "Homage to Catalonia" 2003

Antony Beevor, "The Battle for Spain" 1982

Canal Sur, Andalucia, "Cuentas Historicas" 2013

Gerald Brennan, "South from Granada" 1957

Vicente Navarro, "The Case of Spain" 2008

Spanish Civil War Photography.co.uk, "Anarchism in the Spanish Civil War" 1936

Country Studies US/Spain, "The International Brigades" 2012

US Library of Congress, "Foreign Policy Under Franco" 2008

Spanish Civil War Photography.co.uk, "No Pasaran" 1936

The Olive Press, "Spanish Civil War Communal Graves Located" 2011

US Library of Congress Country Studies US/Spain, 'Policies, Programs and Growing Unrest" 2008

BBC News, "Digging Up Franco-Era Trutha in Andalucia" 2010

US Library of Congress Country Studies US/Spain, "
Republican Spain" 2008

BBC News, "Tales of the Last Survivors" 2010

Carol Macfie Lange, "Talks with Villagers in Andalucia",
2010 - 2014

acknowledgements

THE CONTINUAL PERCEPTIONS AND SUPPORT OF Cristina Parry and Giovanna Rossi Pressley have been pivotal in finishing this book.

Many thanks also to author Sara Banerji and Walton Street Writers Oxford, for valued feedback and encouragement.

This book is printed on paper from sustainable sources managed under the Forest Stewardship Council (FSC) scheme.

It has been printed in the UK to reduce transportation miles and their impact upon the environment.

For every new title that Matador publishes, we plant a tree to offset CO_2, partnering with the More Trees scheme.

For more about how Matador offsets its environmental impact, see www.troubador.co.uk/about/